Books by BA Tortuga

What She Wants

ISBN # 978-1-78651-343-4

©Copyright BA Tortuga 2016

Cover Art by Posh Gosh ©Copyright 2016

Interior text design by Claire Siemaszkiewicz

Pride Publishing

Published in 2016 by Pride Publishing, Newland House, The Point, Weaver Road, Lincoln, LN6 3QN, United Kingdom.

Pride Publishing is a subsidiary of Totally Entwined Group Limited.

WHAT SHE WANTS

BA TORTUGA

Dedication

Dedicated to Julia, who dared me to write a contemporary western ménage that made sense to her and who makes my life a place of joy. I hope I did you proud. I love you. For those of y'all following the Roughstock series, *What She Wants* falls during season two. As it is, I write cowboys as I know them—with all their faults and foibles and weird grammar. All errors are mine and I own them proudly.
Thanks for reading. Readers are what make the world go round. Hee-yaw, y'all!

Chapter One

The bed was a touch too soft, but Adrian didn't mind. He had something warm and hard to curl up to, and he shifted closer to Packer, his traveling partner. That hard hip and broad shoulders gave him plenty of purchase to keep him from sinking too far into the mattress.

Smiling when Packer shifted closer, Adrian pushed a hand down the length of Packer's torso, loving the width of the fuzzy chest and the ridged beauty of the most underrated belly in bull-riding.

He hummed, wrapping his fingers around Packer's rising dick and tugging.

"Morning, you. Did you make the coffee?" Adrian asked. He could smell it, acrid and somehow dark brown, as if the smell itself had a color.

"Naw. I been sleepin'." Packer's Aussie accent was thick as late-summer pond water in his mostly-asleep state.

Adrian raised his head, frowning. "Did it have a timer?"

Packer grunted softly, tugged him in closer, hips moving the heavy cock through his fingers.

"Mmm." He forgot all about the coffee, that velvety skin covering the hardest dick ever making him a little distracted and a lot horny. Adrian started kissing his way down, wanting to give it a fine good morning.

Packer was all for it, too. Adrian could tell. Jesus, he loved the way those tight abs rolled and jerked.

He licked at Packer's belly button, his fingers working the extra skin at the tip of Packer's cock. He loved that foreskin, found it fascinating. Packer moaned low and arched, bowing up toward him, the sheet falling away.

Adrian laughed, blowing air on the tip of Packer's cock before pushing the foreskin back and licking at the head. Salty. Damn.

"Oh, now. That's pretty." A camera flash went off, blinding him.

Adrian shot up on the bed, Packer grunting when Adrian's hand landed hard on his belly. "What the fuck!"

"Oh, don't stop on my account, boys."

Oh.

Oh, Jesus.

Oh, Fucking Hell

He knew that voice. Adrian blinked over and saw Calleigh, his wife, sitting on the chair, a cup of coffee in one hand, a camera in the other.

Packer rose up on both elbows, staring past him. "Well, hullo, Calleigh. What brings you to Des Moines?"

One red eyebrow arched and Calleigh smiled, slow and wicked. "I got tired of waiting at home for someone to give me some attention, honey."

Adrian was completely speechless. His cock wilted. Packer's didn't.

Bright green eyes met his. She was made up—eyes and lips and everything—and she was a fucking wet dream, or would have been if she hadn't been an evil bitch. "I told you, I'm not waiting for you anymore, Adrian. I've been taking pictures for about an hour. If you want me to come along on the road, I'll clear out the memory card. Otherwise, I'll take them to Ace. It's totally up to you."

His mouth opened and closed like a landed fish's. "Come along?"

"Yes. Twelve years we've been together and I've never traveled farther than downtown Dallas with you. I'm done. I want in. I want to play, too."

"Play..." Adrian felt like a parrot. Calleigh wanted to play. She was a hard-working nurse. Lost job or no, he wasn't sure she knew the meaning of the word 'play'.

"You heard me. I'll give you time to figure yourself out."

She stood and he saw her, like it was a dream. Jesus, she was in the tiniest little leather skirt and boots up to there and a tiny, lacy top. "I'm going to get some more coffee. If you want, I'll buy you both breakfast."

"Give us half an hour," Packer said, holding Adrian back when he would have gone after her.

"No hurry." Calleigh turned and walked out, heels clicking on the floor.

Fuck.

Fuck.

Fuck.

Packer turned him, a little rough, a little too fast, that beautiful mouth crashing down on his in a hard kiss.

Wait – What?

His head spun and he groaned, trying to figure out what the fuck was happening here.

Packer kissed him until he couldn't breathe, until his cock was hard again. It was ready to go off like a rocket. Then the man chose to break for air, that amazing smile right there in front of his swimming eyes.

"I swear, Chook, you never told me your wife could be so fucking hot. I might just have to punish you for that."

Christ. His heart slammed in his chest and Adrian wondered when he'd lost control of his life so completely.

He was so utterly fucked.

* * * *

Okay.

Okay.

Jesus.

Calleigh stared at her hands, her fingers shaking violently. She'd done it. She'd done it.

It had been six months since they'd restructured the cardiac department and she'd taken the chance to leave. Six months of spa treatments and personal trainers, shopping and researching, and figuring out how to save her marriage.

If it was savable.

Hell, to find out if it was.

All she knew for sure was that she wasn't going to spend the rest of her life working eighteen-hour shifts in Dallas.

She didn't want to spend her life without Adrian, either. They'd been so young when they'd gotten married. So different. Still, even though she knew he had this whole other life without her, she didn't want to lose him.

And if it didn't work, at least she was trying, pulling out all the stops. Now all she had to do was keep on like she'd started out.

She sat with her coffee for twenty-five minutes, and she was starting to think she was going to get stood up when Adrian came out of the lobby elevator with Packer, both of them dressed, but a little mussed.

Calleigh kept her face schooled, smooth. No stress. No worry. Hold out.

Adrian tried a smile, but it trembled and slid away before it fully formed. "Hullo, baby girl."

"Hey, cowboy. Packer. Are y'all hungry?" She wasn't going to be a child, damn it. She could do this. Adrian had always been honest about his relationship with Packer. She ought to be able to pull this off.

"We are." Packer bent to kiss her cheek, and it made her face heat like crazy. She'd met him, sure, but he'd never really paid her any attention. Not like this.

She stood, letting herself be right in Packer's personal space. "Excellent. Come on."

They followed her like a pair of alley cats, Adrian slinking with his head down as if he was in trouble. Packer was more...prowly.

She kept her chin up, boobs out, focusing on swaying her hips like Jeannie in Zumba class had taught her. They got settled, and she would swear Adrian was flushed. He'd given her that look a lot, once upon a time.

The waitress smiled at her. "The special today is blueberry pancakes and eggs Benedict."

Gag.

"Thanks. Can I have a small glass of orange juice, please? I bet the boys want coffee."

"Yeah. And some juice for both of us, too, yeah?" Packer smiled, and the waitress blinked. Packer had that effect on folks. His looks were misleading, his features rough, not quite matching until he smiled.

Calleigh met Adrian's eyes, forced herself not to feel guilty. Adrian could've asked her to come a hundred times, a thousand. Adrian hadn't even come home in nine months. If he didn't love her anymore, she needed to know.

"You look good." Adrian tapped his fingers against the table, leg bouncing under it.

"Thank you." She held his eyes. "You weren't half bad this morning either."

Now she knew he was blushing—his cheeks went nuclear red. Packer just hooted.

Come on. Come on, Calleigh. Strong. Sexy. Sure. "And you passed inspection, I think," she told Packer.

"You think so?" Packer reached out and patted her hand. "I'm waiting for us to get the chance to do an inspection in return, yeah?"

"If you're good." She hoped she was going a better job of hiding her blush than Adrian. "If y'all decide to let me come play, of course." Not that she'd left Adrian much of a choice.

"Calleigh, what's going on?" Adrian blurted it out finally, which actually relieved her. That he wanted to know. "You've never wanted to be a traveling wife."

Traveling was better than sitting alone at home and getting old. "I told you. I'm young, I'm alive, and I'm tired of waiting for you to remember where the house is."

"I... You were never home when I was anyway." Adrian couldn't make it an accusation, staring down at his hands, his ears red. She wasn't sure he was even trying to make it one. They were pretty messed up. God, this was a terrible fucking mistake.

For real.

Somehow, in her head, it'd been daring and hot and wild and a way to get Adrian's attention. Sitting here in this restaurant, it felt way more like blackmailing your husband and his lover.

His lover who was more sexual just sitting there than she was all dolled up and wiggling.

Jesus.

Calleigh lifted her chin and stared him down, refusing to show how bad she wanted to turn and run. "That doesn't matter. I'm here now. Fucking deal with it."

"Aw now, luv. Don't get all defensive. You've given the lad a shock is all. We can work with this."

Wait. Was that the toe of Packer's boot against her ankle? "I'm not trying to interfere. I want to come along." She was so fucking lonely, so bored. "Play, if you're interested."

"Play." Adrian blinked at her. "I— Who are you? I mean, not that I don't want to play with you." He kind of seemed surprised that he'd said that.

"Adrian, I realize that you haven't seen me in almost a year, but you ought to remember me." She was going for playful, but she sort of meant it.

"I do! You wear ponytails and scrubs and you hate heels." Oh, there was pouty Adrian. She almost smiled. It might be okay.

"I haven't worn my scrubs in a long time."

The waitress brought the drinks, asked for their orders.

"I want the fruit plate, please."

"Do you serve the whole menu all day?" When the waitress nodded, Packer hooted. "The great American burger for him and the pork chop platter for me, please. Ranch on the salad." Packer ordered for both of the guys, then put his chin on his hands. "So, what are your demands, luv?"

"I thought I was pretty clear upstairs." She winked at Packer. Of course, she didn't know if she could sleep with him, or if that was part of the deal or what, but... Yeah.

"That's it? Just 'let me come'? I mean, you have to use

what you have, luv."

"Shut up." Adrian whacked Packer.

She chuckled, sipped her coffee. "I'm not looking for a pity fuck. I'm tired of being alone. We've been married for eight years, and you haven't even tried to come home since Christmas. You rode in Austin, even."

Adrian shook his head, biting his lip a moment. "I didn't know what to say, baby. I wasn't sure you'd want me to."

Calleigh stared for a second, and she sort of knew that she'd fucked up. Bad. "Did you even think about it?"

"I did. I have." Those bright green eyes met hers and he tried that smile again. "This is messed up, huh?"

"Yeah. Yeah, it is." And the guy she'd been in love with for ten years couldn't even smile at her anymore. She grabbed her purse, pulled out the camera, three twenties, and slipped off her wedding ring. She put the camera and the rest on the table. "I wouldn't have really messed up your career, you know. It was less desperate and needy in my head, more sexy and fun."

She got up and walked out, her boot heels clacking on the tile. It felt a little cool, really. Just to walk off without saying goodbye. She told herself that all the way to the twentieth floor, and it kept her from crying the whole way.

"Are you mad, Adrian?"

"Huh?" Adrian turned to stare at Packer, his gut churning. "What do you mean?"

"I mean, you let your wife walk off and leave her ring. She's something else." Packer had gone from smiling and at ease with Calleigh to growly in a heartbeat.

"She is." He actually grinned a little, sort of, then he touched her ring. It was still warm. And tiny. God, he didn't think he'd ever seen it up close. That killed the smile. "Maybe it's for the best."

"Why? You hate her? She's a bitch?"

"What? No. No, she just…" He shrugged. They'd stopped talking somehow. She worked eighty hours a week—he was on the road. She had a stressful career and the house in the suburbs and all—he had Packer and the rides. "She lives a different life."

He didn't hate her. Hell, he didn't really know her anymore.

"Well, it seems like she wants to live yours, now. She's a looker, too." Packer went from growly to…slinky, maybe. Hot as hell. Packer was good at that.

"Yeah. She sure seems different." She seemed like…whoa. He didn't think she knew how to walk in heels that high.

"I noticed. She never looked like that the few times I met her. Not a bit of it. She's working it hard, Adrian. She wants you back."

He pocketed the camera. "What? We're going to let her come along?"

Packer stared at him. "Christ, you're a thick one."

"Oh, fuck off, mate. She was good when I explained about you, but this is… Well, she's here."

"Did you see her legs? Her ass? This is a good thing." Packer thought about everything in the lowest terms. Adrian wasn't sure he could be that easy.

"Of course I saw her ass." *Sort of,* he thought. He'd been more staring at her hair, those boots.

"Well, she's got it going on. You never told me." Packer reached under the table and touched his knee. "You have to think about this. Can you let her walk off like that?"

He sighed, met Packer's eyes. "I can't fucking believe she showed up here. Hell, I don't even know how she got into the damn room." Not only that, but he had to ride tonight.

"She's your wife." Packer stood up, tossing some bills on the table. "You're acting a right wanker, Chook."

"She already left cash, mate." And the food wasn't even here yet.

Damn it.

Things were always getting fucking complicated.

Chapter Two

"'Nother drink, beautiful girl?"

Some pretty-pretty man with pale blue eyes and blond curls smiled at her, finger sliding along her exposed collarbone, and Calleigh nodded. "Please."

She'd cried for an hour, slept for ten, then she'd gotten a massage and a facial. Her flight home wasn't for two more days and she wasn't going to hide in her room, damn it. This was her vacation. The girl at the casino boutique had helped her pick out a new dress—a jeweled, emerald-green halter with a tiny gauzy skirt that showed off her belly button jewelry and the tattoo she'd gotten over spring break. Add that to a great pair of black pumps and stockings that hugged her thighs, and she hadn't lacked for a second of attention.

Her head was up and she'd been dancing with a pair of beautiful Brazilian men before this lovely blond had offered to buy her a drink.

Fuck Adrian. She didn't have to beg for attention, damn it.

Something pretty and pink was handed to her, and she took it, murmuring her thanks.

"Anything, beautiful." That touch came again and she blushed.

That drink went down easily and he took her hand. "Eduardo and Matteo and me, we want to dance with you again."

And off she went. The lights were swirling, the music driving, and the hard bodies around her were all interested. Eager.

Appreciating her.

Wanting her.

It was almost perfect, but almost perfect was good enough. She danced, her head falling back, her arms rising up, and those Brazilian boys could shake it. Hard. Someone lifted her up and somehow she was on a bar, the lights going crazy, and she was moving, hips rolling.

There was hooting and hollering and catcalls, and she closed her eyes, letting the music have her. At least until the world tilted when someone snatched her off the bar, her tummy landing on a broad shoulder.

"Hey!" She beat on a fine, muscled back. "Let me go!"

"No. What the hell are you thinking, Calleigh?" Adrian. It was Adrian.

"What? I was dancing!" She relaxed for about a second, before she remembered she'd left him. "Let me go!"

"You were dancing. You're not now." She bounced when he hefted her to keep her from sliding.

"Careful!" She couldn't kick too much without her everything falling out. "Adrian! You're not listening to me!"

"Nope. Tried that. You walked off." Oh, he was doing the caveman thing really well. His hands were like iron bands around her thighs and that made her a little dizzy, a lot wet.

"Where are we going?" she asked.

"Up to my room." He grunted, when someone almost smacked into them.

"Put me down!" His hands slid up her thighs, and she started wiggling.

The security guard stopped them on the way to the elevator. "Is everything okay?"

"Yessir." Adrian chuckled, sounding completely normal. "She's my wife. She was trying to make me jealous. It worked."

"Ah. Have a good evening, sir." The bastard laughed!

"Hey!" Calleigh tried to breathe enough to talk.

Someone was holding the elevator and Adrian went right in. Adrian smacked her butt a little. "You hush."

She gasped and whapped him back. "Asshole!" God, he smelled good.

A low chuckle sent shivers up her spine even as Adrian rubbed the spot he'd hit. Packer. It had to be Packer who'd held the door.

"What the fuck do you think you're doing? I was having a good time…"

"You were? It seemed like you were taking bids." The bell dinged, and Adrian hit the hallway, her body bouncing with his every step.

"What the fuck do you care? Let me down!"

Packer followed right behind, cock hard, evident in his tight Wranglers.

"Oh, now, you're the one who didn't give me time to even think about things! I want to come with you, she says, then takes off her ring and walks off." Adrian waited for Packer to open the door before striding into the hotel room and dumping her on the big king bed.

She pushed right up, determined to walk back out. Deal with this shit on her own. Cope.

Adrian planted a hand against her chest, the heel of his hand covering her left nipple. "No. We're going to chat."

Her nipple went hard like whoa, and she saw him grin, saw that he felt it. Jesus, that pissed her off. She slapped his hand away, ignoring the way that her top scraped over her breasts, bared her a little. "Fuck you."

"Now you're talking, baby." Adrian grabbed her by the shoulders, yanking her up against him. Then he kissed her senseless, like he hadn't since they were first married.

Oh, god. He felt heavenly, hard and solid against her, one thigh pressing between her legs. She didn't know what to do, but her body did. Her body wanted him to touch her.

He did, too. His hands slid down to push her up by her butt, his hips rolling against hers. He was hard, really hard. For her.

She'd lost one shoe, so she hooked her leg around Adrian's hip, dragging them together. She distantly noticed Adrian's hat flying off, then his fingers found her garter belt, her G-string, and it didn't matter. He shoved her back down against the bed, scrambling between her spread legs. Even through his jeans, she could feel him, rubbing up and back against her.

She growled when the elastic bit of her G-string let go, but his fingers pushed against her, and Calleigh thought she'd make him buy her another pair. Then his thumb found her clit and she arched, heels digging into the mattress.

A rough sound tore out of him, but he didn't ruin it with talking. He kissed her again, his fingers working her, making her want to scream. When he pulled back, she reached for him, but he only left long enough to undo his jeans.

He was still mostly dressed when he pressed inside her, fucking her with deep, strong strokes that she couldn't begin to argue with.

Calleigh couldn't remember the last time he'd been this desperate for her. Maybe he never had been. He was now, slamming into her, his lips latching onto her neck to suck up a mark.

"Adrian…" She was going to scream, it was so big. So hot.

"Yeah, baby. Oh." His skin slapped against hers, his balls pushing at her with every thrust. His hips managed this slip and slide and he was nudging her clit with each thrust, driving her higher and higher and higher. She needed a more. Just a little.

She got it. Adrian yanked her up, sliding against her, his cock so deep inside she thought they'd never get apart again. Calleigh sobbed and shattered, the room spinning as her orgasm flooded her.

Adrian groaned, so rough and low that his chest vibrated against her breasts. Then he came for her, filling her, wet and good.

She rested her forehead on his shoulder, the shirt still smelling like spray starch.

Oh, God.

He never said a word, just stroked her back, his big hand soothing. Warm.

She took a deep breath, feeling like she could for the first time in months. Everything was kind of sparkly and perfect, at least until someone chuckled, someone who wasn't Adrian.

"Oi. You're over each other, all right. Broken up for good." Packer snorted. "My arse."

Packer sat in the most uncomfortable hotel easy chair on earth and watched Calleigh and Adrian scramble to cover themselves. That was right amusing, considering how much he'd seen of Adrian over the last few years.

Finally Calleigh gave up and hightailed it to the bathroom, stumbling along in that tiny bit of dress. Like they were newly met and still deep in lust. Over each other. Adrian had thrown a wobbly about Calleigh showing up, but the moment he'd seen her dancing with the Brazilian boys, Adrian had lost his shit.

Packer stared, one hand on his crotch, rubbing some. Mostly it was an absent movement, but it could have some intent at any moment. They'd gone at it hammer and tongs, his boy and the pretty lady.

Adrian glanced over at him, gave him a half-grin. "Not classy, mate."

"I'm the epitome of decorum, me." Packer shrugged. "You gonna go get her, or are you gonna come get me off, too?"

"I have to pick one?" Adrian asked.

Oh, ho! Some lad had made his mind up, Packer thought. "No. You can do both. Consecutively, not concurrently." He grinned, letting his arse slide to the edge of the chair and spreading his legs.

Adrian's eyes dragged along Packer's body, then he licked his lips and started unbuttoning his shirt.

"Mmm." Packer did love that pretty chest, the ripped abs. Adrian did damned near as many crunches as Joaquim the amazing Brazilian.

Adrian was still raring to go, buzzing, pretty dick filling up again.

Packer's cock jerked as he wondered what Calleigh tasted like. He knew Adrian. Spicy. Almost like there was pepper mixed with the salt. Packer unzipped his jeans, letting his dick free.

He heard the bathroom door open, glanced over to see Calleigh coming out, grabbing her shoes.

"Wait." He barked out the order like he would at any young filly, and she stopped in her tracks. He'd known she would. "You aren't going anywhere. Not after the effort this lad put in to go get you."

Her lips parted and, for about half a second, he could see them, wrapped around his cock, the image so perfect and wonderful. The very thought made his hips roll, which made Adrian moan. His boy knew him. He crooked a finger at Calleigh, banking on her confusion.

She took a step forward, and he admired how that heart-shaped ass moved, side to side, the dangly belly ring catching the light.

"Closer, luv. I don't bite unless you ask me to." He supposed he could put his cock away, but it would be a shame to waste such nice wood.

That made her chuckle and she came a step closer. That brought her arse to where Adrian could see it. He heard the deep moan and knew Adrian had seen that wild butterfly inked across her back again. That glimpse down in the bar had set his lover on fire.

"Good. Now…" He stopped to stroke himself a few times, just to keep things revved up. "I think you need to quit running off without giving Adrian a chance to chat."

"Are you sure you're thinking, Packer?" Oh, ho! Hot and quick on her feet.

"Unlike my mate here, I can think and fuck at the same time." He winked at her, then rubbed Adrian's arm when the lad muttered a protest.

"This is..." She fluttered and Adrian reached for her, stroked her lower back. That got her to arch and those breasts were right there.

Packer did what any red-blooded male would do. He reached out and squeezed. Mmm. Not fake. Soft, warm, firm, and he wanted to see. Good thing for him, Adrian was a smart lad, working ribbons and ties open.

Once the ridiculous excuse of a dress was gone, Packer pulled Calleigh into his lap. Might as well hang for a wolf as soon as a sheep.

Two things happened at once—Calleigh moaned and Adrian moved, shifted to kneel between his legs, hands sliding up his thighs. Such a smart boy. He grinned at Calleigh, pushing his hips up. This was going to be such fun.

"This is probably a bad idea," she murmured. She had a black garter belt on and a soft, pretty belly. Her underpants had been sacrificed to Adrian's need.

"You think so? It was your idea, lovely." He found her ass with his hands, lifting her so he could settle her up against his stomach more, giving Adrian access to his cock.

"I have a lot of bad ideas." Her nipples were hard as pebbles and right there at his lips.

Speaking of lips, there was a pair of lips wrapping around the tip of his dick, working his foreskin.

"I'm all about them. I haven't had a good idea in years. It works for me." Packer bent to lick at one perky nipple, wrapping his lips around it, like Adrian was doing to his cock.

"Oh..." Now that sound Calleigh made was something worth remembering—shocked, hungry, desperate.

She had no idea about hungry. Packer pushed up, giving Adrian more, taking more of Calleigh's sweet body. He might be in heaven. He heard another muffled cry and Calleigh bucked, rubbing against his belly.

"Pretty girl." Packer loved on her, his mouth coming back up to take hers in a kiss.

Oh, soft. Her lips were so soft and wet. Different than Adrian's, which were hot and hard, the suction sweet around his dick.

Packer groaned, letting some of the immense tension out with the sound. He reached around between him and Calleigh, touching her, finding her slick, hot folds.

He also found Adrian's fingers, playing her, stroking. Adrian helped, showing him how to make her fucking crazed while sucking him like a Hoover. Such a good lad, his Adrian. Such a fucking beautiful mouth. Greedy, too. Adrian could suck like a dream. Calleigh was soft and giving and her clit was sensitive as anything.

Happy cries pushed into his lips. Calleigh's eyes were heavy-lidded, but she was watching him, looking at him.

That was important. He needed to know she was with them, that she knew who she was fucking. Adrian gave Packer a hint of teeth and Packer pushed two fingers inside Calleigh's body, wanting her right there with him.

"Oh." She rolled up, stretched tall, then bore down, taking his fingers again.

How in bloody fuck any two people who liked sex as much as these two could have drifted apart, he didn't know. Packer gave Calleigh what she needed, fucking her hard with his fingers. He felt Adrian's groan all around his cock and Adrian took him in, deep, swallowing around the tip of his dick.

"Fuck!" Packer bucked up, his whole body shaking with the need to shoot. He held on, barely, long enough to press his thumb over Adrian's, grinding against Calleigh's clit.

He felt her come, her walls trembling and shaking against his fingers, squeezing him tight. There. Packer gave it up, shooting right across Adrian's tongue, and the relief was fucking astonishing.

Adrian pushed behind him and he felt that hard cock, nudging his fingers, wanting back in Calleigh's body. Lord, that girl was going to ache so good in the morning. And this was just night one.

Packer helped, lifting her right up, hoping the chair would hold the three of them. It rocked, but stayed upright, and Adrian's rough thighs felt fine against him.

Her breasts slid against his chest, warm and soft even through his shirt. Her lips were on his throat, open, wet, breath huffing out of her. Packer held her, spreading her for Adrian, letting the lad have her. His cock was pretty well spent, but it felt good to have them rubbing.

Adrian's gaze met his over Calleigh's shoulder, dark eyes flashing, hot.

Packer hummed, keeping one hand on Calleigh's butt. He used the other to press behind Adrian's head, pulling him over Calleigh's back for a kiss.

Adrian tasted like him, salt and male, and, fuck, it was fine.

Every thrust Adrian made rocked Calleigh into him, her mouth hot on his skin, her skin so soft compared to his and Adrian's. His cock threatened to rise again, so he reached around and pinched Adrian's ass.

Adrian grunted, hips jerking restlessly, the kiss getting sloppy and wet.

He bit Adrian's lip, wanting to feel it when Adrian came. Now. Fuck, yeah. Yeah, that was hot. Adrian slumped down, trapping Calleigh between them.

Packer held on, trying to keep the laughter inside. It came out as a light chuckle anyway.

"No laughing, mate. Chair'll bust." Adrian's eyes were rolling a little.

"Well, then, Chook, move us to the bed." That seemed logical, yeah?

Calleigh laughed, shook her head. "I should go to my room."

Adrian's smack was loud, and Calleigh jumped. "Be still, now. You're staying. Right here."

"Mmm." Packer grinned. "You're so over each other."

"Fuck off, Packer." Calleigh pinched him but good. "I'm still mad."

"Uh-huh." He met her eyes, grinning huge. "You should have seen him, luv, when he saw you with the boys from Brazil."

"They were hot."

Adrian gave her another hard swack.

"Ow!"

"Chair won't hold up to that, either." Packer reached past Calleigh and gave Adrian a bit of a shove. "Bed." They could talk there.

Adrian nodded and stood, hauling Calleigh up and holding her as one hand was held out to him. Packer took it, feeling a little creaky when he got up, but his cock was still half-hard, so it was all good. Happy-making. Almost as happy-making as the way Adrian got them all naked, lickety-split, and in the bed, under the covers.

"Better?" Packer snuggled in, happy with gratuitous nudity.

Adrian chuckled, Calleigh caught between them.

"I thought so." They'd have to talk, all of them, but especially Calleigh and Adrian. That could wait a bit, though. Sleeping together was like communing or something.

Something hot.

Chapter Three

Hot.

It was hot in here.

She hummed, stretched, sliding against...

Wait.

Wait.

Whoa.

Calleigh's eyes popped open and she met Packer's eyes. Oh, God.

Oh, God.

She'd...

They'd...

All together and... Oh, God.

"You're panicking, baby." Adrian sounded so sleepy.

"I..."

His hand slid over her belly, warm and heavy and familiar.

"Shh." He moved a little, snuggling in, like he used to on Monday nights when she'd have to go to work and he'd gotten home Monday morning. They'd spent whole days together in bed.

She let her eyes fall closed, and she hummed happily. She loved him. She loved him so much.

"I have your ring, baby. I want you to put it back on."

She turned her head, stared at him, frowning. "Are you sure?"

"Yes." He sure seemed certain. She knew that face. It was the one Adrian wore right before he nodded his head, right before the gate opened on the bull he was about to ride.

She opened her mouth to say something smart, but he took her hand, slipped the ring back on her finger. Then he kissed her, which sorta made the whole talking thing redundant. He melted her butter, left her dazed and moaning.

His kisses still made her head swim. She'd been so scared that they wouldn't anymore. She turned and pressed close, and slid her fingers up Adrian's chest.

He made a deep, happy sound, pushing into her touch. "We could get breakfast in bed."

"I could eat. Yesterday was all coffee and vodka."

"Gross." The word came from her other side, where Packer had been watching them, keeping to himself.

"Which part?" She was naked beside the man and she didn't know if he drank coffee.

"Well, I like coffee. And vodka, come to that. I like food more, though. I'd get all acidy and squish all day."

Calleigh rolled her eyes. Boys.

"Yeah, then he'd walk around all day asking, 'Oi, who opened their lunch?'" Adrian said, rolling his eyes, too.

"Adrian, that's nasty." She popped his hip, shook her head.

"What?" Adrian pulled back to stare. "He would."

"Still, y'all. Nasty fart talk." She ran her fingers through her hair, wincing at the crunchiness of it. "I think I need to clean up a little."

"Why? You smell good." Packer was just... She'd thought Adrian was bad with the boy stuff. Packer nuzzled her neck and she shivered, reaching for Adrian.

"It's okay, baby." Adrian kissed her, loving on her.

Packer was solid behind her. Adrian was hot in front of her. She met her husband's eyes, needing to know this was right, real.

He smiled, dropping a little kiss on her lips. "Only what you want, baby."

She wanted to feel, to know. "I want," she said.

"Good." Packer said it against her ear, his lips moving on her skin.

She gasped, electricity slipping down her spine, and her

fingers curled. "Oh."

"So pretty, baby. I'd forgotten..." Adrian had the good grace to look a little ashamed.

"Try to remember now, huh?" She'd worked so hard to make herself fine for him, to make him recall how good they could be.

"I am. I am remembering." Adrian kissed her again, mouth hot and firm on hers.

Packer backed away, eased her down on her back, then she was trying to keep up with a wild, three-way kiss that threatened to burn her alive. They were so pretty together, so overwhelming. Hot as fire and twice as dangerous.

Somebody was easing her thighs apart, somebody was teasing a nipple until it ached. Adrian licked a path down her belly. She'd know that touch anywhere, anytime. So it had to be Packer at her breast, lips moving strong on her skin.

"Oh, y'all..." Her hands fluttered a little, because she couldn't think fast enough to put them anywhere.

"Come on, love." Adrian was always helpful that way. He showed her where her hands could land, one on his skin, one on Packer's. She curled her fingers in Adrian's hair — with her other hand she explored Packer's shoulders, tracing one ropy scar after another. Bull-riders.

Packer chuckled, like he was reading her mind. "I'll tell you all about them, luv," he murmured against her skin. His lips caught her nipple again as Adrian spread her legs wider. Fuck, this was insane.

"God, baby." Adrian bit her, a tiny sting of teeth.

"Damn..." Her back bowed, shoulders and hips pushing into the mattress.

"Sweet." Packer was talking, too, hot as hell.

Adrian wiggled between her thighs, tongue sliding up along her slit, so hot. She didn't know what to do, who to move close to, who to rub on. Adrian had the best mouth...

"I..." She didn't know how to say this was big without Adrian stopping.

"Shh." Packer worked back up to her mouth, pressing his against her lips. That way she didn't have to say anything. She just had to relax and let it happen. Packer's tongue sliding into her lips, parting them, the motion heady, stealing her breath. He was a much harder kisser than Adrian, much more demanding. As opposed to coaxing or asking.

She gasped and he groaned, pressing even harder. She pushed back, giving Packer back a little. He laughed against her mouth, the sound one of pure joy. Adrian bit her thigh, his teeth making her gasp. Calleigh arched, and Adrian bit again. Oh, fuck. Hot.

Such a toothy man. When had that happened? She'd bet Packer had taught him that. The thought was really exciting.

Packer's hand slid down her belly, fingers tugging the dangling navel ring just enough that she groaned. That made Adrian grunt and start sucking up a mark on her thigh.

God, they were a tag team from hell. They moved like they were weirdly in tune. It made her shiver, made her shake. She reached out, fingers barely brushing the tip of Packer's cock. She was curious, wanting to get it, to know how he felt.

There was such soft skin there, and she had to push at it, just to feel it move. It was kind of amazing. Packer made a deep sound, so she did it again. And again.

God, that was hot.

Not as hot as Adrian's tongue slipping over her clit, though. Fuck. Adrian smiled against her skin, letting her know how pleased he was with her reaction. She could read him even when she couldn't see him.

"Don't stop, please, Ades."

He licked again, then backed off, blowing a stream of air over her folds.

"He's a right tease, isn't he, sweet? Are you a tease, too?" Packer pushed against her fingers, hard and needy.

"No. I take what I want." Now. She was tired of waiting.

Adrian licked and she bit her bottom lip, thumb working the wet tip of Packer's cock, the slit slick. "Fuck."

"That's it, girl. You need to take what you want." Packer was like a shoulder devil or something, the voice of naughty.

She reached down with her hand, the one that wasn't incredibly busy exploring Packer's cock, fingers tangling in Adrian's hair, tugging him closer. Adrian moved for her, his cheeks pressing against the insides of her thighs, his tongue working her clit mercilessly.

"Oh. Oh, fuck. Right there…" She turned her head, lips open, hunting skin.

She got it, Packer moving right in to kiss her again, his lips rising up from where he'd been nibbling on her shoulder. She moaned, working Packer's cock, her entire body burning. They were making her crazy. Packer shifted a bit, still moving into her hand, but shifting around so he could touch her, too. His fingers found her right where Adrian's mouth did.

Oh, fuck. Adrian was licking her, licking Packer's fingers, which were flicking her clit, and she was on fire. They were so in sync, so attuned that they had like a mind meld or something. Their mouths moved at the same time, Adrian's tongue pressing into her as Packer bit her lower lip.

Calleigh's breath hitched and her thighs started shaking. Fuck. Fuck, she was going to…

"Come on, sweet. Now." The 'now' came with a twist of Packer's fingers and a push of Adrian's tongue. Then she was flying. When she could focus again, Adrian was kissing Packer, cock sliding against her.

They were both moving, slow and easy to begin with, hips rocking. The wet sound of their kiss was insanely erotic. She reached out, sliding her fingers over both of their chests. Both so different, but so hot, so male.

Packer was fuzzy. Adrian waxed. Vain man.

She gathered the drops of salt at the tip of Packer's cock, licked her fingers, curious to know if Packer tasted different. Different, but the same, really. She tasted her fingers again.

"God." Adrian had turned to stare at her, his eyes like fire on her skin.

She moaned, wet her lips, tugged the tip of Packer's cock again.

"Fuck." Packer slammed against her and Adrian, thrusting faster all of a sudden. Probably because now he had the undivided attention of both her and Adrian. She scooted down, pressing hard against Adrian's cock even as her lips wrapped around the tip of Packer's dick.

"Christ on a pogo stick." Packer bucked, panting hard.

"Oh, fuck, baby girl…" Adrian eased into her, making her toes curl, and she started sucking. They all moved together again, like they were in perfect concert or something. The sounds and smells made her want to explode.

Packer got one hand under her neck, supporting her, and she opened eagerly, taking more. Packer was never a bit tentative. The man knew what he wanted, and he took it. He pushed into her mouth, slipping as far in as she could handle.

Adrian cried out, and his hands were everywhere, pinching and stroking and petting and making her crazy. All the while he was driving into her, the little ache perfect. It had been so long. So long, and this was like nothing else, ever. Crazy. Insanely hot.

She saw Packer grab Adrian and tug him in for another kiss, watched how Packer devoured her Adrian out of the corner of her eye. She was — oh God, she was going to burst, explode into thousands of tiny little pieces. She pulled on Packer's cock, pinching one of her nipples, driving herself higher.

"Baby." Adrian gasped when he broke the kiss with Packer, grunting, driving into her.

"Please." She was right there. Right fucking there.

"Yeah. Come on, Chook. Make her come." Packer was moaning these filthy things, touching her, and Adrian moved faster. Harder.

It was all she could do to groan and suck the tip of Packer's cock for a second before she was soaring, her nerves firing like crazy.

So good.

Packer grunted above her, his cock rubbing against her lips. Adrian was still hard in her, too, still moving. Calleigh could focus now, though. Thank God. She pulled Packer into her mouth, legs dragging Adrian in deeper.

The boys both cried out, touching each other, touching her. She felt powerful, knowing they were both depending on her for their pleasure. Knowing they were both right there, wanting her.

"Come on, baby. I need..." Adrian's eyes crossed when she squeezed him, his breath coming out in a huff as he went off like a rocket, deep inside her.

Then she got one hand under Packer's balls, squeezed. His whole body went tight, his cock pushing in deep. She could feel it when he tried to pull away and be polite, but he couldn't manage it.

Calleigh took him in, focusing on the deep, rough cry, on the way Packer called out her name. Okay. Hot.

"Lord have mercy." Packer panted out the words, and she felt a surge of pride. She'd done that.

Adrian settled her back, lips covering hers, and it was weird for about, oh, a quarter of a second, then it was hot again. Adrian didn't let it be anything but hot, and when Packer's fingers slipped between her and Adrian to touch her, she almost went into orbit.

Her hips started moving again, getting her clit the right amount of pressure. Packer, though, the man was a fucking tease, making her arch for it, work for it. He was evil. Later, she'd like that about him. Right now she wanted him to touch her. She moaned her need into Adrian's lips and his response was to roll his hips, tug her bottom lip between his teeth.

They were working her together. To heck with tag teams, they were simply a team, well-oiled and making her want to scream. "Fuck. Please, y'all... Don't stop." She was flying and didn't fucking want to come down.

"Not going to, baby." Adrian laughed against her mouth. "Packer can go all night."

"It's a long time till ni—"

Packer's fingers tweaked her clit and she bucked, thoughts flying out of her head. Adrian hummed against her skin, pushing down against her, pressing Packer's fingers down. Hard.

She shuddered, wave after wave of pleasure crashing through her.

"You can do it, baby. You can give it up." Adrian bit her, right at the base of her throat where people could see.

Her whole fucking world shattered into, oh, a million pieces, leaving her limp, panting like she'd run a mile. Adrian and Packer were both smiling at her when she finally touched down, a little smug. She could live with that for what they'd done to her.

"Morning." She couldn't fight her own grin, not at all.

"Hello, luv." They said it together, and she had to snort.

"Heaven help me," she murmured. Although Calleigh thought heaven wouldn't have a hell of a lot to do with this, right now.

* * * *

Packer stretched, pondering a shower. He did a couple of side-to-side stretches, then dropped into one of those yoga things. The dog exposing his balls or what have you. Maybe he could take a shower. Leave Adrian and the little woman to sleep away the morning. Wasn't that a kicker, the way she'd shown up? Packer liked her style.

He heard someone slide off the bed, that pretty sheila dropping down into the yoga pose, easy as you please.

Packer grinned. Look at her. Gravity was kind. He chuckled. "You gonna lead us in some practice, luv?"

"I could. I took classes at home." She winked over. "At least your hands are busy like this."

"Are you worried about my hands?"

A soft snore came from the bed. Adrian had no stamina.

Calleigh chuckled. "I think I ought to be. They're clever."

"I like to think so. They like you well enough." He followed her lead into something that made his sore shoulder feel like it might fall off, then the muscles released enough that he groaned.

"Is that a good sound?"

"Yeah, luv." It was the first time all that pressure had given up in ages.

"Excellent." She stood up, headed over, fingers sliding over his shoulder, the touch warm, firm. "No swelling."

"Nah. S'just sore as a boil. Always is." She talked about his hands? Hers were like magic. Those fingers dug in, finding the sore like that, pressing in until the fool muscle gave it up.

"Oh, God. That's good," he moaned.

"Settle on your butt, let me see." She pushed him, then started rubbing and touching. Packer's eyes crossed, partially from the touching. Partially from the nipples bobbing right there in front of him.

She was certainly less self-conscious than she'd been last night. Woo. Course, the gal was a nurse and was in full-out healing mode. He reached out, fingers meeting her belly, the little dangling ring-deal in her belly button.

A tiny gasp escaped her, and her eyes came up to stare into his. Packer grinned wide, feeling kinda big bad wolf. He tugged, real easy, wanting to know how it felt. He got his answer, straightaway, when Calleigh's pretty hips rolled, curls brushing his thigh. Nice. He nodded his approval and tugged one more time, pondering where else she might be sensitive.

That time the arch got her breasts right in his face, nipples hard and dark and right close for a delicious, fucking heartbeat.

Packer did what any man would do. He bent and licked at one.

"Oh." She arched again, and he grabbed her, giving her his arms to bend over.

That whole yoga thing came in handy then, because she could press back and put her tits right where he needed them. He pressed his face against her and breathed deep. Man, he did love the scent of a woman — so different from a bloke. Not better, but fine, and not what he normally got.

She was soft, too, her breasts sweet, her nipples hard as little stones. He turned his head, got one between his lips and started sucking. She was sweet as honey, this one. Packer could see why Adrian had gone for her, could see why he'd never let go even when he was confused as hell.

Packer eased her closer and got her straddling one of his thighs. She was wet and hot as a flame, pushing down and rocking on his leg in time with the pulls on her nipple. A fucking firecracker, this one. So neglected. Packer figured that was partly his fault, so he'd help a girl out. He held her down with one hand, playing with her breasts with the other.

"This is..." She arched, sliding on him, pretty as you please. "I didn't come down here to do this."

"I know." Bullshit he did, but it didn't matter. They were doing it now. And he would do it again. Fucking was the only thing more fun than riding bulls. "It's okay," he murmured, in case she was worried.

"Shit, it's better than okay."

Oh, that made him hoot. Tough, beautiful broad. "There's more, I reckon." He lifted her, rubbing on her belly.

"Mmm..." Her eyelids got heavy, the makeup smeared by her eyelashes, the expression rough, slutty, hot.

He did like his women a little on the trashy side. Just like he liked his men to bottom and suck. Packer thought he might have stumbled into a beautiful fucking relationship. He kissed her throat, licking the mark Adrian had left there. Hoo.

Her head fell back, long red hair damn near touching the floor. Pretty. So fucking pretty. Packer ran one hand down the center of her body, tugging that tiny ring again. Her lips parted and she bucked up, curls tickling the tip of his cock.

"Fuck." That felt so good that he pushed against her, his dick sliding along her mound.

She shifted, wet folds hot along his shaft.

"Christ." His teeth ground hard, his jaw set as he tried to get control.

"Do you do girls, Packer?" She rubbed over the tip of his cock. "Or are you boys only?"

"What do you think, luv?" He pressed against her again, just to be sure she felt what he was sporting.

"I think." She sank down on his cock, taking him in deep, just like that.

"Oh." His neck arched, his hips rolling, his hand clenching under her ass. He needed to get a solid grip because his world was spinning.

"Yeah…" Fuck, she was tight around him, muscles gripping something fierce. And when she started moving… Heaven. Someone had been doing her Kegels. God love her.

Her lips found his ear, little breathless gasps making him shake. He wanted to babble, but he figured it would be loud, and he didn't want to wake Adrian. Yet.

One hand found his nipple, long nails teasing, pinching.

Hips bucking, Packer moaned, panting. "That's it, luv. Like that."

Calleigh nodded, tongue sliding on his ear. "Like this?" That sharp pinch came again.

"Just like that." The touch had him all but dancing, his body rocking. She rode hard, like he was a rank bull and she had nothing else to do, ever. Packer gave as good as he got, his legs straining, his belly hard as a rock. He held them both up, letting her ride.

She bounced, a dull flush climbing up along her belly as her tight pussy squeezed him. She was so pretty that he couldn't get why Adrian would up and leave. It had made sense back when they first met, but now… Packer needed to talk to the lad.

Later.

Much later.

After he wore this beautiful girl out. Grinning some, Packer nibbled at her throat, just under the bruise. God, that was stunning. He felt how much she liked that, all around his dick. Moaning, Packer moved fast and hard, ready to get the ride going strong. He was done playing.

"Oh…" Her hands framed his face and she curled forward, kissing him hard. She was damned good at that. Made a man a little crazy, in fact. Damn. Her tongue matched the rhythm of their bodies, even as that sped up, started to fall apart.

Packer shook a bit, trying hard to stay upright, trying to keep up with the hungriest woman he'd ever met.

Her hot cunt rippled around his dick, the muscles going mad around him. His breath heaved, his muscles quivering under his skin. He held on until he knew she'd found her pleasure, though, letting her ride it out.

"Your turn." Sweet, giving girl—she rode him hard, teeth stinging his bottom lip, just enough to make him wild.

Packer almost fell on his bum, but he managed to come and shout and hold her up all at the same time. He was a stud.

Lazy, slow applause filled the air. "Very pretty, mate."

Calleigh's cheeks went a dark, dark red, and she turned to gape at Adrian, who watched them with heavy-lidded eyes.

"Mmm. She is, huh?" He wasn't gonna let her hide, not from him and Adrian. "She's a good one, this woman of yours." He took her mouth again, slow and easy, making sure Adrian got a good show.

Sometimes Adrian needed to be reminded about what was good in his life, right? The lad could be dense. Packer heard Adrian slide down from the bed, the man's heat rubbing on his back.

Oh, fuck. He might get it right back up. That felt so damned fine.

Adrian's tongue traced his ear, hand sneaking around to press between them and head south.

"Greedy." Packer chuckled, his hands clenching on Calleigh's ass. Her skin was so soft compared to Adrian's, so sweet.

"Mmmhmm. You two started without me."

"You were sleeping, Adrian. Hard." Calleigh's words were all gentle-like, careful.

"S'okay. I liked what I saw." Adrian was sweet as pie, too. Packer figured he might get a cavity or two being around them.

Of course, her tight body shifted on him and Adrian bit him, hard enough for a sting. That was way more like it. Grunting, Packer started shifting back and forth between them.

"You want to go again? Impressive." She leaned and kissed him, then Adrian tilted her head, took a kiss of his own.

Adrian's chuckle sounded breathless and horny. "Pack is always impressive, baby."

"You're not bad, baby." Calleigh reached out, fingers wrapping around Adrian's dick. "Not bad at all."

"Thank you." Adrian bucked against them, and Packer grinned. So easy.

Adrian tugged at the dangling jewel on Calleigh's belly button, and Packer's eyes rolled. Damn. Damn, he could feel that, buried inside her.

"You—" He tried to talk, but he couldn't get the words out.

"Yeah…" Adrian rubbed against his hip, cock leaving burning trails on his skin.

"God." They were gonna burn him alive. He was quickly learning that singly they were like flames, but together they were a blaze.

Her kisses were softer than Adrian's, but deeper, longer, each kiss lasting until he thought he'd scream with it. Fucking A. Packer moved a bit faster, letting them have at him.

Adrian slipped behind Calleigh, one hand dropping down, touching where he was buried in that hot cunt.

Christ. His whole body jerked, his nerve endings singing.

"Somebody likes that, eh, mate?"

"I think it's more than like." Calleigh sounded smug.

Packer reached around, swatted her butt. "Watch it, girlie."

Calleigh gasped and started bouncing. That was it. He had to keep them off balance. Off balance and hungry. It was a fine plan.

He might survive this after all.

Chapter Four

Calleigh finished lining her eyes, then started on her lips. Dinner out. With the boys. Like out-out. At a restaurant. One that had steaks and lobster. Adrian had made the reservations and Packer had promised to pick her outfit — which, okay, terrifying — and leave it out on the bed for her.

The wonder-Aussies were going to the hotel spa for a massage and shave. Jackasses.

When she came out of the bathroom, the outfit was indeed laid out on the bed.

Calleigh'd never worn the dress before, never. She'd seen the little A-line fringe number in a window in Dallas, the copper sparkle lighting up the storefront. Somehow it didn't surprise her that Packer had chosen it.

Add to that the six-inch pumps and a pair of dangling diamond earrings she'd never seen before, and she felt like a Barbie doll. It was remarkably modest, really. The dress had beaded straps and a scoop neckline with a deep plunge in the back. It came well below mid-thigh, but somehow she felt more exposed than she had in the mini she'd worn the night before.

She found a pair of seamed stockings and a black garter belt, easing them on, smoothing them over her thighs. There. She looked good. She knew it. She needed to stop worrying about it.

Sparkly clips went in her hair, perfume went into the hollow of her throat, and she grabbed her clutch, heading down to meet the boys in the lobby, on time, thank you very much. Adrian was always late. So it must have been Packer who had them in the lobby, waiting for her.

They were hot as hell—both starched and pressed, hats on. Packer's belly was tight as a board under the navy blue shirt, and her Adrian's eyes were burning as they stared at her.

It was Adrian who came and kissed her lips lightly, taking her arm. "You ready, baby?"

"I am. Do I look okay?" She shimmied a little.

"You look amazing." His smile said she was better than that. She hadn't seen that expression so much in years.

Her cheeks heated, her heart fluttering. "Thanks. Y'all look like a slice of heaven."

"You think so? I'd have gone south." Laughing, Packer moved close, fingers brushing her back above the fabric. "You're like a really good sin."

Her nipples tightened, and so did her belly. "Feed me, boys. I'm starving." She'd been doing a ton of core work, so she knew she looked good.

"Mmm. All that exercise." Adrian's grin widened.

She offered him a quirked grin, a nod. "You know it. I rode hard." No shame, damn it. She could keep their interest.

"Cowboy-ed right up, luv." Packer chuckled again, which stirred the hair at the nape of her neck.

"Mmm. Be good, now."

They led her out to the valet stand, where a sexy black pickup waited. Someone's hand brushed the curve of her ass as she walked.

"We're very good. You ought to know that, baby." Adrian handed her up into the truck. Packer drove.

She ran her fingers over the leather seats and hummed softly. She did love a tricked-out truck. This one had to be Packer's. Adrian's was red. Hers was champagne-colored.

Adrian chuckled, and Packer blinked over at her, one eyebrow raised. "What? I like a nice truck."

"Good." Packer's voice held a wealth of satisfaction. "We'll have to test out how much later."

The sun was down, the lights buzzing by, and Calleigh felt light, free, like she was heading for the top of a roller coaster.

"So, you like steak or lobster better, luv?"

"Steak. I admit it, I'm a meat eater." Lobsters were messy, anyway.

"She doesn't like butter fingers, Pack." Adrian pressed up against her. He'd refused to sit in the back.

"This is true. Well, it's okay at home, with an old T-shirt on." She leaned into Adrian's warmth, snuggling.

"Oh, now, at home you should have someone to feed it to you."

Adrian's fingers slid up her thigh. "At home, mate, we can think of all sorts of things to do with this beautiful body and buttery fingers."

Oh. Oh, damn.

"Oh, hell yes." Packer patted her other leg, his fingers lingering.

Adrian explored the lace band at the top of her stockings, then the garters. Then skin. She waited for the groan—her Adrian loved stockings, loved the access of garter belts and thongs.

"Oh, fuck, Calleigh. You know that makes me crazy."

She gave Adrian her best innocent expression, but it was derailed a little by Packer's exploring fingers.

"Nice, luv. Didn't know it was a hot button of Adrian's."

Another groan sounded, this one a little rueful. "No, but he'll use it now. He'll buy you a thousand pairs."

She laughed, leaned over to kiss Packer's jaw, just barely. "You and I have to talk, darlin'. Compare notes," she said. "I think we could make him crazy."

"Oh, I know we can. He's so easy, huh?" Packer's fingers slipped farther than Adrian's, the man that much more daring.

Her breath caught, and she nodded, her thighs sliding.

Adrian chuckled softly. "Careful, mate. She shaves when she wears these. Makes her sweet and slick."

"Oh, Christ."

They were going to steam up the windows the way they

were all breathing hard. "Y'all need to be good now." She let her leg rub against Adrian's, let her thighs part a little wider, to tease them all.

"Mmmhmm. We're always good. With you I bet we could achieve greatness." Adrian's pinky touched the crease of thigh and torso, making her gasp. They were like newlyweds, but better, the heat between them deeper, fiercer. Packer was this amazing, fiery presence, too. Just waiting, like a big predator.

They pulled into a parking lot and Packer parked toward the back. The silence as the engine was killed was huge.

"Well. We have a reservation, luvvies, so in we go." Packer kissed her under her ear, his arm going around her back so he could reach Adrian's arm.

Adrian chuckled, nodded and they tumbled out, Adrian making sure she was steady on her heels. She could see the way heads turned so people could stare, and she loved that all the women in the place looked jealous. They should be.

Adrian held her chair for her, her fringe tickling her thighs as she sat.

The waiter smiled at them when he came, handing her the menu first, but giving Packer the wine list. "Can I get you something to drink, folks?"

She smiled at Adrian. "Are you boys having beer?"

"Yeah, I think so." Adrian grinned back. "What have you got in a nice dark ale?" Adrian settled on a local brew and Packer managed to get a Victoria Bitter, which she knew from experience was actually an Aussie pilsner.

She went with a nice dark red, knowing that it made her lips shine.

They all blinked at the menu, but she had to laugh, because the toes of their boots found her feet at the same time. Boys.

"What looks good?" She wanted a little steak, a salad. Maybe some shrimp.

"Oh, I like the Porterhouse." Adrian always had a hollow leg or something.

"Not the grilled chicken breast salad?" She couldn't help

teasing. She'd fed Adrian chicken for the first year she cooked for him.

"Oh, God. You'd poison me if you could." He grinned at her, tapping her leg with his foot. "I need my red meat protein, as hard as I work out these days, baby."

Packer snorted and Calleigh chuckled. "I bet you get your fair dose of…protein," she said, arching a brow.

"Oh, he can have as much as he likes." Packer's grin went evil-evil. Lord, he was hot when he smiled.

"What about you, sir? Are you a chicken man? Shrimp?" God, this was fun.

"Oh, I like a good shrimp, now. With steak." Packer almost chortled. "Like a good loin, too."

That made her giggle. "Poor me. Neither one of y'all are breast lovers."

"Now, love, don't count us out on that. We're not as fond of chicken."

"He's got a point, baby girl."

"Duck? Goose? Ptarmigan?" What the fuck was a ptarmigan anyway?

"Wife." Adrian's hand covered hers, squeezing.

Her cheeks heated, and she grinned. "Well, then. I suppose you boys deserve your red meat."

"There you go." Sometimes Adrian sounded like a Texan. If Texans had that weird lilt to their voices.

She ordered the petit filet and a salad, along with the shrimp cocktail. Whatever she didn't eat, someone would. Adrian got his Porterhouse, and Packer got some surf and turf thing, and over the first round of drinks the man had her and Adrian laughing like loons about some beach story that involved Brazilians and crabs.

She countered with a story about Helena's wedding out on Lake Texoma. "Y'all should have seen her, dancing around on the boat in those heels. When Gordon tripped and they went over the side, it was like the funny video show."

She'd been Helena's matron of honor, just like Helena

had stood up for her with Adrian.

Adrian shook his head. "I didn't know Helena had gotten married."

"Lord, she's pregnant with baby number two. I'm Bethany's godmother. She's a hoot." For a second she thought about the life she'd walked out on—house, land, friends, job. Then she glanced at Adrian, who was staring at her with that mixture of awe and love and a little shamefacedness, and she couldn't think of a reason not to be right where she was.

Her hand found his knee, touching him, and she couldn't help but smile.

Packer took a long pull of beer before clearing his throat. "Why no kids for you?"

She squeezed Adrian's knee again. "I had a miscarriage early on, but nothing since. It's just not in the cards." Hell, that was why they'd gotten married.

"Sorry, luv." Packer patted her leg in return, and Adrian reached out to grab her hand. Cowboys. American or Aussie, they were all the same.

"It's okay. I work long hours... Worked, I mean." She probably didn't have time to be a mom.

"How's the wine, luv?" Packer adroitly changed the subject, squeezing her knee.

"Rich, wonderful. I'll have to drink slow or it'll go to my head."

"Oh, we can't have that..." Her two men grinned at each other, talking in unison again.

"Which part? Drinking slow or getting tipsy?"

"I like the way you think, you know." Packer was about to start something, she could tell. Something raunchy maybe. Thank goodness the appetizers came. She nibbled on her shrimp—of course, so did Adrian.

And Packer.

They also made their way through lobster fondue and toasts and some salads. Those boys were storing away some energy.

Adrian's steak came, and it was the size of a brontosaurus. "Good lord. Are we feeding the Flintstones?"

"I'm starving, baby girl. And Packer? He may be wiry, but he can eat. No worries."

She shook her head, grinned and cut her little steak up. "You two are going to be comatose later."

"I'm not the one who falls asleep after a half a slice of cheesecake." Oh, now Adrian was playing dirty.

"No, but chocolate and coffee leave me wired for sound, Meat Boy."

"Mmm. She has a point."

"Yeah? Chocolate and coffee for dessert, then."

She looked over at Packer, grinned. "Are you sure you can handle me wired for sound?"

"I think we can, love. It may take two of us." Pack's eyes were sharp, serious, and the expression made her wet, made her nipples ache they hardened so quickly.

Adrian gasped next to her, and she knew he could tell where she was headed.

"It'll be fascinating to see y'all try."

"You have no idea. You caught us by surprise before, right, Chook?"

Adrian nodded. "Packer is good with a plan."

She sized them both up and decided her best chance to get a leg up was Adrian. "I bet he has lots of plans with you."

Adrian's cheeks went an adorable shade of pink. "Usually, yeah."

That made her chuckle, feeling back on top of the game.

"Now I get to include you, hmm?" Adrian's hand slid up her thigh under the table. She hadn't even noticed how close he'd moved.

"Be good, now." Her thighs parted, she couldn't help it.

"There's no fun in that, love." Packer's fingers sent chills right up her spine.

Her belly went tight and she ached, wriggling a bit. "Don't make me beat you."

"Oh, no. We'll do that to Adrian."

Adrian gasped and her eyebrow went up, her lip quirking. "Will we, now? I haven't done that since before we were married," she murmured. They had only done that twice, when they were young and wild and testing limits.

Packer moved even closer. "Do tell, love. We need to compare notes."

"No. No, you don't."

She glanced over at Adrian, then Packer turned her to face him. *Okay, whoa hot.* "Hey."

"Hey. We're talking about the plan. Pay attention, luv." Packer winked, and he was so close she could count individual lashes.

"Are we? I'm an RN, you know. I'm very good at following a plan."

"Mmm. You have a good knowledge of anatomy, too, I reckon." That smile... It fascinated her.

"You have no idea, mate." Adrian made her grin when he sounded a little panicked.

"I do. I love when he's crazy for it, too." Calleigh knew Adrian could do amazing things, when he needed.

"Yes. When he's twisting and burning and his ass is a little red, huh?"

Adrian made this noise, half outrage, half horny, that made her and Packer both laugh.

"Yeah. He wouldn't let me, after the first couple times. Still, I like when he begs for it." She could push it, she knew it. Fuck, the worst that would happen was that Adrian would retaliate, make her desperate, which—come on—there was no bad there.

"I'm sitting right here." Adrian must have kicked Packer, as his foot disappeared and Packer grunted.

"Sorry, Ades." She crossed her legs and focused on sipping her wine.

"No, you're not." He chuckled, the sound warm and fond. "Besides, I may have some plans of my own." His hand slid down her back, tracing the line of bare skin to her tattoo. His fingers traced it and Calleigh shuddered, shivered.

"You have to share, too, Chook," Packer said.

"Do I, now? Because I have a wee advantage, eh? I know where you both need to be touched, mate."

She was going to set aflame.

Packer's laugh had a husky note to it now, and she could feel his body shifting restlessly. "You do. I bet there's a hundred things you want to try, too."

"Maybe a hundred and three. The small of her back makes her twist. I can't believe you got a tattoo there."

She shrugged. "The artist was convincing."

"How convincing?" She had expected Adrian to growl, but it was Packer who got huffy and growled at her.

"Convincing enough that I have a butterfly now." She arched an eyebrow, stared Packer down. "He promised me, if I breathed through the first bit, I'd love it by the end." She had, too. She'd been full of energy for hours.

"It's hot, huh?" Adrian got it. There had been no bad touching. Just the buzz.

"I was stoked, yeah. Slept on my belly for a week, though."

"Adrian slept that way for a few days the first time he and I got together."

Oh, God. Just the thought of that made her want to squirm.

She licked her lips, eyes on Packer's. "I bet it was hot as hell."

"Fuck, yes."

"Are we interested in any dessert?"

They all started, then looked at the waiter. Like they'd all forgotten they were in a restaurant.

"I…" She blinked, chuckled. "I don't think so. Boys?" She was interested in dessert that involved that hotel room and way less clothing.

"No, thanks." Adrian had enough presence of mind left to smile at the man. "Just the check, please."

She nodded, checked her lipstick. "We can have coffee and chocolate up in the room."

"We can. We'll order, then make Adrian stay dressed until it comes." Packer stood, heading off to hunt down the waiter, obviously too impatient to wait for the check to arrive.

She blinked over at Adrian. "You okay, Ades?"

He was flushed, eyes hot, hard as a rock in his good jeans.

"I'm on fire, baby." He stroked her back, his fingers hot as hell on her skin.

"I want you. I want to play." She leaned in, breathed into his ear. "I'm aching." She was also a great big horny slut girl.

"I love you. Fuck, you and Packer are making me ready to come in my pants."

She touched the curve of his ear with her tongue. "Don't you dare. That's mine. *Ours.*"

His body shook a little. "I'm trying, baby girl."

"God, I can smell you." She rested her cheek on Adrian's shoulder, watching Packer stalk back across the restaurant toward them.

"And I can feel how you're squeezing your legs together."

"You two behaving?" Packer asked, putting a hand on both of them.

"Not a chance. You ready? I deserve coffee and chocolate."

"You do, luv. Come on." Packer guided them out, close as a second skin.

The fringe on her dress moved, tickled her thighs where it brushed her. They piled in the truck again, Adrian against her side. She turned halfway, begging a kiss, a touch. Something.

She got it, Adrian's arm around her waist, his mouth coming down on hers. Oh, God. Yes. She cupped his jaw as Adrian tongue-fucked her lips, and he slid one of his hands up the outside of her thigh.

Adrian moaned, moving even closer, almost knocking her back against Packer.

"Driving, Chook. Careful."

She nodded. "No wrecks." She leaned back against Packer a little bit, though, her bare back on his arm.

"No. We're too busy," Pack said, sounding definite.

Adrian chuckled, nodding along, licking at the skin beneath her ear. That made her moan, the hot spot sending pure heat to her cunt.

"Love that. When you moan for me."

Who was this amazing, seductive man, and what had he done with her husband? She couldn't be more pleased with her plan.

"Are we almost there?"

"Hell, yes." Packer spun them into the parking lot of the hotel, finding them a place to leave the truck.

They tumbled out of the pickup, Adrian stealing a hard kiss as he helped her out of the truck. Packer muscled up behind her for a few seconds, rubbing against her ass nice and hard. God, they felt amazing. Pure sex.

"Inside." They staggered some on the way in, and she knew everyone would think they'd been drinking.

"Y'all celebrating?" A bitty red-headed cowboy with a stacked, Bettie Page-looking lady waved at them.

"You know it, Cotton. You have a good one, mate." Packer waved, but kept on going.

She heard a soft giggle, but it didn't matter. Adrian's hand was on her lower back, fingers circling and making her gasp. When they got into the elevator, she stepped away. "Ades, that's making me crazy."

And wet.

"Mmmhmm. And this is bad?"

Packer took over, touching her feather-light. "This, you mean?"

"Hey!" Her back arched, nipples aching where they brushed her dress.

"I never play fair, love. Come on, Chook. Let's go make her crazy."

The elevator door opened and they headed for the hotel room. She'd brought her bags up this afternoon, let her single room go. They got her inside the door, got it closed and locked, Adrian joking about how Cotton might tell someone else with a C name and that could be bad...

"Do you two have another girl who's going to be jealous, now?" That thought hurt a little bit, okay, maybe more than a little bit, but she didn't let it show.

"Nah, love. He was saying Kynan might try to bust in and catch us in the act. That's a boy. And we're not fucking him."

Adrian shuddered. "Oh, mate. Way to ruin the mood."

She bent over, slipped out of her heels. The action had her mouth near Adrian's cock, ass bumping Packer's leg. "Three is enough."

"Three is good." The zipper at the side of her dress let go, and the boys pulled it off her when she straightened. That left her in stockings, garter, and a tiny G-string, hair up, and feeling incredibly naked.

Adrian stared at her, licking his lips, eyes hot as fire. "Baby..."

She flushed dark, then Packer's finger stroked the top of her panties, tracing her shaved mound, and she thought she was going to die.

"You're a wet dream, love." Packer moved in, his finger moving the scrap of lace aside. He kissed the skin below her ear.

She went up on tiptoe, rocking slowly. "Oh, damn."

"Mmmhmm. Ah-ah-ah, Chook. You have to call room service. Hands to yourself," Pack reminded Adrian.

Oh, that was mean. Hot, but mean. "I need chocolate and coffee, Ades." She met Packer's eyes, winked.

"And Pack will want fruit." Adrian grinned, obviously willing to play along for now. She wondered how hard Packer intended to push.

"And it'll be cheesecake for you." She knew him. At least she hoped so.

"It will." Adrian got the menu and called, and Packer took advantage of the distraction, pulling Calleigh close for a kiss. His clothes rasped all along her body, making her gasp, groan, her nipples sliding against him.

His hands felt just as rough, his calluses catching on her

garter. He was as tall as Adrian, maybe taller, which was big for a bull-rider. He cupped her ass and he lifted her, just a bit, his jeans rubbing against her.

"Such soft skin."

"You're not soft." Her hands landed on his shoulders, and that moved her nipples against Packer's shirt again.

"Nope. I'm hard as can be for you, luv." She could feel him, even through his jeans.

"Kiss me again?" She was feeling the barest bit buzzed.

"I can do that." Packer kissed her again and before it was done Adrian was pressing against her from the other side.

Adrian's fingers met Packer's, squeezed them, then eased down her thighs, stroking her through the stockings. They were driving her crazy already and she still had no access to skin. That wasn't fair. She had the feeling if she complained they wouldn't feel the least bit sorry for her.

"Here, luv." Packer caught her hands, pulling them up to his chest. "Let's get me all naked, too."

"Excellent idea." She started working buttons open, trying her best to ignore the hands sliding over her skin.

Adrian was hard to ignore, though. He knew all of her hotspots. Not only that, but Packer was a viciously fast learner, paying attention to every gasp, every shiver. No wonder he'd seduced Adrian into trying something completely new and crazy. The man was a demon.

Calleigh did her best to fight back, hands working open Packer's belt, easing down the zipper and teasing all the way down.

Packer made these great noises, too, a little bit groan, a little bit growl.

"Oh, you're getting to him, baby," Ades said.

"Good." She let her fingertips trace Packer's dick, the heavy shaft pressing against his briefs.

Grimacing, Packer pushed forward, his hips rolling.

"Just think how you'll feel, sliding against me, all smooth and shaved," she said. When they both moaned, Calleigh felt thirty feet tall.

They all worked on Packer's jeans and boots, then he pushed her back toward the bed. He laid her out, still in garters and all. She pulled the clip out of her hair, tossed it aside. It would poke her in the head.

Packer eased himself down next to her, his cock rubbing on her hip. "Hey, luv."

"Hey." She turned toward him, eyes flashing to Adrian, just making sure this was okay.

Adrian watched them like they were the best kind of porn, shifting from foot to foot. He nodded a tiny bit, his eyes crinkling up. Packer's hand wrapped around her thigh, drawing her leg up and dragging it over Packer's. The G-string didn't hide anything and Adrian's moan made her flush.

"God, mate. Are you sure I have to wait for the food?" Ades asked.

Packer chuckled, the sound pure evil. "Yes."

"We could get into a lot of trouble in half an hour." Hell, they could make Adrian insane in that short of time.

"Oh, luv, you have no idea. Dying to taste you." Packer's fingers walked up her skin to settle between her legs.

Adrian stumbled forward, she could hear him, but her focus was on Packer—on the words, the touch. "Are you now?" She almost didn't gasp.

Almost.

"Mmmhmm. Wanna? Adrian will watch like a good lad." Packer spread her out, slipping down.

"Oh, fuck." Adrian sounded like he'd swallowed a frog.

Her G-string was no obstacle—Packer slipped the tiny thing down, leaving her mound framed by the black lace of the garter and stockings. Packer smiled up at her—that grin completely transformed the harsh planes of his face.

Calleigh winked, reached down and ran her finger down the line of his nose. It traveled to one side, an old break making it crooked. It was fascinating. When her finger slipped off the tip, Packer nipped at it, the bite making her laugh and exclaim, "Toothy!"

"Oh, God, baby. You have no idea." Adrian moved closer to the bed, staring hard.

Packer chuckled, waggling his finger. "Stay there, Chook."

It was amazing, how Adrian stopped in his tracks. She'd have to explore this further. Soon. Right now, though, Packer was kissing his way down her belly, licking under her navel. Her abs went tight and her hips rolled, bumping up against Packer's chest.

He made that amazing growly noise of his and grabbed her hips, holding her down on the bed. "Don't worry, luv. I got you." Then he bent and put his mouth between her legs, licking and kissing.

"Oh..."

His chin was perfectly rough against her freshly shaven mound and the softness of his lips, the heat of his tongue, was shocking.

Packer opened her with his fingers, his tongue slipping and sliding against her clit. Oh, God, it had been too long since someone had done this.

Her toes curled and she stared up at Adrian, one knee bending to spread, to offer Packer more. Adrian's eyes were like a touch of their own, making her feel so sensual, beautiful. Wanted.

He licked his lips, opening them to say something, but the damned phone rang, cutting him off.

He stormed over to the phone and Calleigh's focus landed back on the man driving her out of her mind. His tongue teased her clit, over and over, and it made her thighs shake.

Packer's hands weren't exactly still, either. The man was pure devil, knowing just where to touch without any instruction on her part. Some men weren't into going down on a girl, but some... Fuck, yeah. Calleigh groaned, loud enough that Adrian glared from where he was talking on the phone.

It made her want to cackle. She didn't have the breath with Packer sliding two fingers inside her.

"Oh..." She rose up on her elbows, her hips encouraging

him to keep up, to let her have more.

A low chuckle vibrated against her skin, more felt than heard. Adrian slammed the phone down.

"Fucking room service."

"Ev... Oh, fuck..." She rocked as Packer's fingers hit a hotspot inside her and her hips bucked. "Everything good?"

"They have rotten timing." Adrian came to loom over them, almost reaching for her.

"Ah-ah, Chook." Packer raised his head a fraction. "You be good and I'll give you a treat later." Adrian groaned, that heavy cock thick and hard in his Wranglers, and Calleigh moaned, moved on Packer's fingers. "Good boy. And girl." Packer bent back to her, his tongue rubbing her mercilessly.

"Oh. Oh, please." Calleigh couldn't fucking breathe and she tangled her fingers in his hair, pressed him closer.

"Mmm." Packer didn't tease anymore. He licked and sucked and fucked her with his fingers, his breath so hot on her it almost burned.

Her back arched when she climaxed, her heels digging into the mattress. Every inch of her felt awake and alive and tingling.

"Beautiful, huh? Such a pretty sheila." Packer moved up to kiss her belly, then sat up. "Come here and kiss me, Chook. Get a little taste."

Adrian all but pounced Packer, their chests slapping together as Adrian devoured Packer's mouth.

Oh, fuck. Hotness.

Packer grunted, hands going to Adrian's back, holding him in place. Adrian was wild, humping, moaning, but Packer finally pushed him over.

"Not yet."

Adrian growled softly and Calleigh's nipples went so hard they hurt at the expression on his face, all need and frustration.

Packer stood up, bumping chests with Adrian, backing him away from the bed. "Chocolate. Coffee. Yeah?"

Adrian's fingers cupped Packer's cock, rubbed hard

through the jeans. "Yeah, mate."

Shuddering, Packer pushed against Adrian's hand. "Yeah."

Calleigh chuckled. They were such boys. Such hot, horny boys.

"Oh, are we ignoring you, love?" Packer kissed Adrian one more time, hard on the mouth before slipping down next to her. "Can't have that."

For a second, she thought she might be in a bit of trouble, having that focus on her. Then she decided the ride was going to be worth it.

"You all right, luv?" Packer was watching her closely.

"I am." She scooted closer, let their bodies touch.

"Good. Adrian is no pussy. He'd let us know if he wasn't happy." Packer kissed her throat, his tongue flicking at her skin.

"Right by her collarbone, mate. There's a hotspot that won't quit."

"Don't give up all my secrets, Ades!"

"Why not, baby? He'll find them eventually."

"Maybe." She laughed as Packer's teeth scraped against her, heading toward that sensitive spot.

"Definitely." Packer said it against the hollow above her collarbone.

Her breath actually caught in her chest, just hitched, and Calleigh's hips rolled toward Packer's heat.

"I like to find the hotspots." Packer did it again, his hand on her belly.

Her hips slid, the garter belt shifting.

"I think there must be one here, too." He stroked her belly, low down, above her mound.

"Oh..." One leg drew up, her inner thighs damp with her need.

"Sweet lady." Packer kissed her, stroked her.

Adrian's fingers slid up her legs, catching on the stockings.

"Careful, Chook. You have to be able to get the door."

Adrian was wicked. Adrian's hands were so damned

warm. "I'll get the fucking door. I can smell you both. Makes a man hungry."

"Like it when you're hungry, Adrian. Makes your hands shake. Makes you all flushed and hard." Packer's fingers never stopped moving, taunting her even as his words taunted Adrian.

Fingers slid along her slit, and she wasn't sure whose they were, but they slipped through her folds, nudged her clit. Then another set met the first there and she had her answer. They were both touching her.

She sank her teeth into her bottom lip, breaking the skin as her hips bucked up. Packer's mouth found one nipple, worrying it, and electricity slammed through her belly. They were going to make her explode. She was going to die of terminal pleasure.

"So fucking hot, baby girl. All pink and wet for us."

Oh, God... No talking. Ades' voice had always made her stupid.

"Look at that. Keep talking." Packer licked at that spot on her collarbone, his fingers working her good.

"Mmm. I do love you shaved, baby. Love how soft it makes you, how sensitive."

"Shh..." She tossed her head and she could feel her tension ratcheting up again, tugging at her belly.

"Why? I think you need to come for us again, baby girl. I think I want to see that," Adrian murmured.

"Ades. Y'all..." She stretched up, restless, skin too hot.

"Shh." Packer's thumb rubbed her clit insistently.

"Fuck. Oh, fuck..."

"Come on, baby. Look at you. You're so fucking hot."

"Sweet." Packer licked at her and Adrian's fingers spread her, slipping inside her as Packer worked her clit.

Her hips rolled up uncontrollably and she almost pulled away from them as the pleasure spiked. They held her down, damn them, and gave her nothing to do but ride the pleasure out. Fingers plunged in and out of her, her clitoris was stroked and nudged until she burned. When Packer's lips found one of her nipples and latched on, all she could do was call out as the world exploded.

"That's it, baby girl. That's it." Ades moved back, letting Packer take the brunt of her shivering and shaking. He never once let up watching her, though.

She didn't even move when room service knocked on the door. Adrian chuckled, went to answer, and Packer covered her up, just in case. Good Packer.

Ades didn't let the waiter in—he took the rolling table, signed the receipt, and locked the door. "Look, baby. Coffee and chocolate."

And oh, it smelled good. She hummed, leaned up on her elbow, rubbing against Packer's side. "Yum."

"Mmmhmm. Look at Adrian. He's all pointy."

"He is. It's a good look for him." She could lick Ades all over, from his mouth to his so-hard cock.

"It is. I like it." Packer swept the sheet aside. "Chocolate, Chook."

She reached down, intending to slide out of her garters. She'd feel less exposed completely naked.

"Oi. I thought you said Adrian liked these." Packer's hand covered hers.

"I did."

Adrian chuckled, sliding his fly open. "I do. Leave them on, baby girl."

"Chook thinks he's been a good enough boy to join us, luv." Packer sat up, hand on her belly.

"Does he now..." She leaned over, let her lips trail over Packer's side.

"I think so." Adrian's pants dropped to the floor.

She hummed softly, licked her lips. "Pretty Ades."

The shirt followed soon after, and she wasn't the only one reaching for Adrian when he slipped down on the bed, holding a plate of chocolate cake.

She scooped up a bit of icing, popped it in her mouth. "Oh, God."

"Share?" Ades leaned in close, mouth closing on hers.

Calleigh slid right against Adrian's chest, letting him have his taste. Adrian kissed her like a starving man, and she didn't think it was chocolate he wanted. Not a bit. Packer's hands were on her hips, thumbs sliding over her ass, encouraging her to move, to rock back and forth between them. They were enough to melt her brain. She was in so much trouble. She'd really had no idea when she decided to come after them.

Their lips separated with a pop and she went for another finger full of chocolaty goodness, offering it to Packer.

He sucked it off, his head bobbing a little. Adrian moaned, watching that.

"Is it good?" She licked her lips.

"It's yummy." Packer kissed her, letting her taste this time.

Adrian pushed into the kiss, his mouth coffee-flavored as their lips all moved together — licking and moaning, tasting. She couldn't breathe. All she could do was feel and touch and need. Her skin felt too tight. She found Adrian's dick with one hand, the other tangling in Packer's hair, holding their lips together.

The boys started moving in concert, as if they knew exactly what rhythm to go on. Beautiful assholes. Calleigh rocked with them, her nipples hard, the ache moving through her body.

"What do you want, Chook? Huh? You want inside her?" Packer was working on making her love his voice, too.

"Fuck, yes. Need you, baby girl." Adrian's hands wrapped around her hips, moving her like she didn't weigh anything.

They positioned her so she lay on top of Packer, his cock against the small of her back, her legs spread wide. Her hips rolled, teasing Packer as Adrian settled between their legs.

Packer's breath huffed out, his body moving under hers. Adrian didn't waste any time, pushing inside her, loving on her. Calleigh made sure she kept moving, keeping Packer with them, driving herself on Adrian's cock. She could feel Packer's heat against her ass, could feel the little drops of pleasure that left his body. Adrian was a familiar width and length inside her, and hot as a brand.

Jesus, it was hot between the two of them. Every inch of her was touched, heated.

"One of these days, luv. One of these days we'll both be inside you, making you scream." Packer whispered it in her ear.

Oh, fuck. She could imagine that, imagine the heat, the stretch, the burn, and that made her move faster, heels digging into the mattress now.

"That's it, baby." Ades had no idea what Packer was saying, but it didn't matter. His blue eyes blazed down at her, happy and horny and all hers.

"Y'all..." Her body started to tighten, the muscles of her belly rock hard.

"Love." Adrian was the one calling her love, now, and she knew he meant it, that he was telling her for real.

Calleigh nodded, found him a smile. Yes. Yes. Love. She tilted her head, got her lips on his chin.

"Mmm." Packer moved faster against her. She moaned, eyes on her Ades. She wanted to watch Packer take him, wanted to see Packer's heavy cock with Adrian's lips wrapped around it.

Adrian grinned for her, bending to lick at her mouth. "You have this look."

"What look?" She squeezed his cock. If he could talk that well, she wasn't doing her job.

"I — oh. Evil." A flush crawled up his chest to his throat, and he bucked against her.

"Just imagining." She was good at imagining.

"What?"

Packer humped hard. "I bet I can guess."

"Try me." Fuck, she was close.

"You like me and Adrian touching, luv." Oh, he was good.

"Yes. Y'all're hot. So fine." And she got to play with them. Like, as much as she wanted.

"You're hot and wet and entirely lovely."

Flatterer.

She moaned, wrapping one leg around Ades' hip. Adrian moaned back, his hips pushing against her pelvis. Her ass rocked back, slid on Packer's cock. She was caught between them, suspended in the most amazing web of pleasure. Her spring was winding up so tight.

Packer's fingers touched her hips, touched Adrian's fingers, and that was all she wrote. Her orgasm barreled down on her like a runaway freight train. Packer rumbled, his hips snapping, wet heat sliding along her back. Ades grunted, hips restless and bucking furiously for only a few heartbeats.

Then her Adrian came for her, too, hard and deep and so good.

She moaned, eyes heavy. No sleeping, though. There was chocolate.

And coffee. Not cheesecake.

Chapter Five

Calleigh sipped her beer, pretended to watch the short go, but she was watching Packer and Adrian get ready. Both of them had ridden yesterday, today. They were looking good.

Adrian was fixin' to ride second to last, Packer was in the lead, and the announcer was already going on about the Aussie invasion. She liked to think that she'd had something to do with that. She'd followed them to two events — played and laughed, teased and goofed off. It had been amazing.

They'd accepted her with open arms, too, which she hadn't been so sure would happen. Adrian had told her a long time ago that Packer was a generous lover, an open, happy man, but she had to admit she was a little amazed.

Adrian was slapping his face, bouncing up and down, focused on the bull. Packer was wandering, whistling lazily. A redheaded cowboy said something to Packer, and he burst out laughing, which was wow.

"Adrian looks good." One of the buckle bunnies with a bun in the oven smiled over at her.

"He does. Thanks."

"Hope he rides."

Yeah. So did she.

"How long have y'all been married?" the girl asked.

"Nine years."

"Wow. Forever…" The little girl pinked a bit. "We thought he was divorced. You haven't been around."

Calleigh arched an eyebrow. "No. I was working. I got laid off."

"Oh. I'm sorry. I mean, I didn't mean…" The girl dropped

her eyes and Calleigh almost felt sorry for her.

"No big deal. It's fun, to get to see the guys."

"Kath, leave her alone, huh? She's got enough on her hands."

"On her hands. In them."

"Girl's got to be exceptional."

"On her knees, anyway…"

Calleigh whirled around, damn near falling on the risers to try to see which of the jealous bitches had spoken against her. There were a slew of them, glaring down at her like a jury, but she refused to let the harpies win.

So what if she was loving on both of them? Who were they hurting?

She watched the gate open, Ballbuster whirling out, Cotton on his back. The bullfighters were jabbering, calling in the background, keeping the bull focused.

Cotton made it to seven and a half seconds. Then he popped right out the back, his hand blown out of the rope. She clapped for him, a touch disappointed, but not totally. It would rock if Adrian took the event. There were three more riders before Adrian, and wow, one of them went down hard. That always took the wind out of the sails. The crowd got all quiet.

Calleigh chewed on her bottom lip, praying a little.

Please let Adrian be okay.

Adrian bounced and bent, holding the rail and dropping it like it was hot. Which it was. He never looked at her, but Packer did, one eyebrow lifted as his eyes dragged over her cleavage, her tiny tank top.

Whoa.

Nipplage.

Packer's grin this time was slow and evil. Damn him. Then he turned on his heel and went to pull Adrian's rope. She leaned forward, eyes on the chute. This was the best part—the scariest, sure, this is where things could go so wrong—but the leather, the resin, the rope, the pulling and straining.

Yum.

There was talking, too, which she'd never noticed. Once Packer had pulled the rope and stepped back across the chute, one of Packer's hands stayed on Adrian's chest, and the man talked a mile a minute. Right into Adrian's ear.

Adrian's teeth bared, the expression the most masculine, sexy thing she'd ever seen. At least in hours. Packer let go, Adrian put his mouthpiece in, then her Adrian nodded, the gate swinging open like a shot. The bull was solid, spinning out into Adrian's hand. She counted under her breath. "Two, three, four."

Eight. Oh, thank God. Maybe it wasn't as good as Packer's ride, but it was a high score, no doubt.

"I think he's gonna do it!" The gal beside her was bouncing, and Calleigh's fingers were crossed.

"I hope so." She grinned over. The kid was pretty sweet, really. The scores came up and Adrian's ninety-two tied him with Packer. The lights went crazy and Adrian bowed to the clown in the middle of the arena.

She bounced up, clapping hysterically.

That was it. Adrian and Packer were going to split the night and Adrian was going to win the event. Oh, God. It was good to be her. Adrian glanced up into the stands, winked at her, and she waved. He was grinning from ear to ear and looking hot as hell.

She headed up with the crowd, knowing full well the guys had to make nice, sign autographs, shake hands. She'd be in the way and she could have another beer. She'd wait for them. Adrian would call her cell. Which had just beeped with a text. She slipped to one side, out of the way, and checked it.

It read, *Woo. We win.*

She chuckled, texted back. *Aussie Aussie Aussie.*

Adrian sent back, *Oioioi CU soon.*

Every event he texted her. Every one. She patted her phone, slipped it back in her purse. Her phone beeped again, about the time she let go. One eyebrow arched as she checked to see what Ades wanted.

It wasn't from Adrian. It was from Packer. It just said, "Soon pretty lady."

She looked across the arena, searching for Packer. He stood back, watching her, and she smiled, nodded. "Soon. I'm ready," she sent.

She could see his sudden grin, the thumbs-up, and she had a feeling it was going to be a good celebration tonight. Calleigh got a few random congratulations, then she headed down to where she knew they'd be waiting for her. She gave her name to the security guy and he waved her through into the crowded maze of cowboy hats and jeans that was the riders' room.

She got a couple of waves there, too. She had known a lot of the wives, but a lot of the ladies she'd known had husbands who weren't on the tour anymore.

It was always a little weird, being the wife of the Aussie, being the working wife. Being the wife with no kids. She didn't get much time to dwell on it, though. The riders started trickling in, some of the ones she knew stopping by to congratulate her. She did a lot of nodding and smiling, did a little grinning as some of the wives commented on how she'd toned up, changed her hair. She wasn't sure if it was admiration or jealousy, but she'd take it.

"Hey, lady." Packer didn't call her luv in front of the crowd, but that was okay. His expression said it all.

"Pack." She went to him, hugged him. "Congratulations."

"Thanks." He hugged her back and rubbed on her a bit where no one could see. "You want to go to dinner with us and skip the bar?"

"Yes." That was easy.

"Good. I need to go change, but I didn't want you to run off." He winked, kissing her cheek before turning back toward the concourse.

She freshened her lipstick and leaned, waiting on them. At least she did until she heard, "Well, Calleigh Roberts. I heard you were here, but I thought for sure it was a lie."

Brandy Collins, head of the I Want To Fuck Adrian But Can't Club and daughter of Adrian's biggest sponsor. Goodie.

Calleigh bared her teeth. "Well, now you can apologize to whoever you were maligning."

One perfect eyebrow went up. "Oh, I'm sure they'll forgive me. Everyone does. Why aren't you cleaning up blood and puke again?"

"Because I'm here, watching my husband win." Little bitch.

"Oh. You're not separated, then."

Calleigh was going to slap the little—

"Hey, baby girl. You ready?" Adrian had changed, but not showered. He smelled like sweat and animal, but it wasn't unpleasant at all. He nodded tersely to Brandy.

"Yeah, Ades. You did so good." Calleigh lifted her face for a kiss.

"Thanks, baby." He kissed her hard enough that her toes curled. Hard enough that she barely heard Brandy huff off.

She blinked up at him, swaying a bit. "I... Hi."

"Hi. Better? You were looking grumpy." He took her arm and turned her toward the exit, ignoring the hoots and hollers. Cotton he flipped off.

"I'm good." She found herself tucked in the crook of his arm, held close. "Packer said dinner instead of the bar."

"Yeah. No one will miss us, really, and we'd rather not share you."

Oh. Oh, wow. "Sounds perfect, Ades."

"Good." His hand slid down to the top curve of her butt. "Don't get me all hot and bothered here, now."

"Why not?" He leaned close. "I won't leave you hanging."

"Ades..." He got her so revved up.

"Mmm. I'm so glad you came to the event, baby girl."

"Thank you." She let him pull her into the shadows, set

them together. "It's been good, to see you, sleep next to you." Fuck like bunnies.

"Yeah. It's been real good." Adrian kissed her, his mouth hard on hers, his tongue demanding entry.

He pushed his thigh between her legs, rocking up into her, and Calleigh moaned, hips rolling in time. God. He could get her off, just like this. Adrian knew it, too, damn it. He was smiling, kissing her neck, her chin. Asshole.

"Evil tease."

He let his thigh move, side to side. Oh, fuck. "Not teasing, baby girl. Well, I might be teasing me, but you get to come." His leg pushed up against her, then backed off, over and over.

She panted against his lips, a dull ache building in the pit of her belly.

"God, baby. You're so good. I could eat you up." He nipped at her earlobe, like he needed to prove it.

"Driving me crazy." Close. She was so close.

"I know. Just think how it will be later, when Packer has his mouth on you."

"Adrian..." She slammed their lips together, her orgasm hitting her hard, making her shudder.

Adrian moaned into her mouth and held her while she shook, his hands like steel on her skin.

"Tch-tch-tch. Chook, look at you two, not waiting on a man." Packer slipped in behind her, kissing her neck. "You come so pretty, luv."

"Ad... Ades' fault. Oh, y'all."

"All Adrian's fault, and I missed out. I might have to punish him later."

Adrian groaned and Calleigh's lips parted. "Can I play, too?" she asked.

"Absolutely. I think we'll make him pay and pay." Packer pressed against her, letting her feel him.

She rocked back and reached out, touching Adrian's lips. God, she loved him. Adrian smiled against her fingers, sweet as anything. Her man.

"We need to get out of here, y'all. Feed my event winners."

"Mmmhmm. Come on." Packer pulled them apart, laughing when Adrian groaned. "Be good, Chook."

Her fingers brushed his cock as she moved. "He's good."

Packer laughed out loud. "He's always good. Just wait. It will get even better."

She dared to cup Packer's balls, gently, quickly. "Promise?"

Packer grunted. "Fuck yes, luv. Fuck yes."

"Excellent." She hooked her arms in theirs, feeling beautiful, sensual, loose in her bones. It was amazing what walking out with the two hottest men at the event would do for a woman's ego.

* * * *

Packer figured taking second was okay, but if he had to do it, he might as well come in second to Adrian. Look at that man strut. Packer grinned. The event was over, they didn't have to ride again for a week, and Packer had plans for that ass.

They'd had supper, Calleigh's choice. She'd settled on barbecue, which Packer approved of. All that finger licking. Now they were on their way into the hotel and Packer was ready for the next course.

Adrian had been teasing Calleigh — tickling and playing, making her laugh, making her sparkle. God, they were pretty together. So fine.

"You two want a beer or..." Calleigh's hand cupped his ass, squeezed.

"We've got some in the room if we need 'em." No way was he losing the momentum they had.

"Cool." Her hair was coming down from the heavy ponytail, strands framing her face. His fingers itched to touch it, and as soon as they were in the elevator, he did. Packer pulled the elastic free, letting her hair spill out.

She blinked up at him from the thick mass, smiled, and

Adrian hummed. "Love the way your hair smells, baby girl."

"Just good shampoo."

"Bah. Some people don't smell right." He goosed her ass.

She squeaked and jumped, breasts rubbing against his arm.

"Mmm. You now, you're like Adrian. You smell good."

"He does smell nice." She leaned back, almost in a back bend, and kissed Adrian's chin. That rubbed her sweet body along his leg, her pussy hot through the jeans. Christ, she was flexible. Woo. Packer watched, pushing his thigh up to give her more leverage. One more kiss and the elevator dinged, and he lost the damp heat against him.

Damn. Still, they were almost to the room, then they would tear Adrian's ass up. He goosed that, too. Adrian rumbled at him softly as they headed down the hall.

"Mmm. Don't worry, Chook. I haven't forgotten what we promised earlier." He'd been delighted when he found out that Adrian was the tiniest bit kinky. And terribly into ass play. Add that naughty sheila to the picture and Packer was in heaven. The door clicked shut behind them, and everyone sort of paused, waiting to see what came next.

Then Calleigh leaned down, slipped those amazing heels off, giving them a long look at her ass.

Adrian made a little noise and started toward her, but Packer stopped him. "Ah-ah, now. You're in trouble."

Adrian arched an eyebrow. "In trouble? For what?"

"We told you before dinner you were in for some punishment." Hell, Packer couldn't remember what for.

Calleigh chuckled softly. "Although punishing him for making me come in the arena may not work in my favor in the future."

No, no. It was for not waiting for him. That was what the punishment was for.

"It was because you started without me, Chook." He grinned when Adrian's face fell, acknowledging that he had a valid point.

Calleigh leaned in close, whispering something low into Adrian's ear, and his boy turned a dark red. Wicked woman. Packer was tickled she'd come to play.

"Strip for us, Adrian." Packer loved it when Adrian was naked and he was still clothed. It made things a little uneven, a lot warmer.

Calleigh hummed softly, the sound pretty and musical as fuck.

Adrian was crimson in the face and neck, which was a good look for him. Then his lad obediently started on the buttons on his starched shirt. Calleigh went to him, took Adrian's wallet and watch, his belt, fingers touching him along the way.

Packer crossed his arms and spread his feet a little for balance, like he would before a show. He watched carefully, taking in every detail.

Calleigh was still in jeans, a tank top, her hair loose, and she looked fine, taking Adrian's good shirt, hanging it up for them. She took Adrian's jeans, too, folding them over, then she skinned Adrian out of his undies, letting her hair brush his skin when she helped him step of them. He did like her style.

She even kissed the tip of Adrian's cock as she stood, Adrian's cry deep and hot as fuck.

Packer grinned. "Very nice, luv. Come here, huh?" He held out a hand to her.

She moved like a fucking wet dream, her nipples hard for them, lips wet and a little swollen.

"Hello, luv." He pulled her close when she took his hand, kissing her deep.

Adrian moaned, and he made it good, his hands framing her pretty little arse. She was soft, yet firm, and he almost distracted himself from Adrian with the feel of her. He heard Adrian take a step forward, a step closer.

"Ah-ah." He held up one hand to fend Adrian off. "I think someone is feeling neglected."

"Well, that's not good." Calleigh turned, smiled at Adrian.

"I think he deserves attention."

"What sort?" He knew what he wanted. Packer wanted to see Adrian's ass glow.

Calleigh glanced over to him, unsure for the first time.

He winked. "No worries, luv. Let me show you how wild he can get. Turn around and bend over, hands on the bed, Chook."

Adrian looked at him, mouth opening and closing, and it was Calleigh who nodded, spoke. "Come on, Ades. Pay attention."

Adrian stared at her a moment, too. Then that fine mouth snapped closed and Adrian moved, bending over the bed.

Calleigh hummed, eyes trailing over every inch of skin. "So fine."

"He is, isn't he? Have you ever seen his ass take on the most beautiful color?"

She shook her head, her pretty hair falling around her. "I want to."

"Pack…" Adrian's protest was low, deep.

"What, Chook?" He knew Adrian loved it, knew Adrian fantasized about Calleigh doing it. "This is right, us."

"Do you want me to go grab a shower, y'all? Give you some privacy?"

"No, love." Packer pulled her toward Adrian. "He's told me that you play sometimes. This is a little more hardcore." He put her hand on Adrian's ass. "His skin is amazing."

"He's stunning." Calleigh's hand moved over Adrian's butt, nails trailing on it, leaving tiny lines.

Adrian went up on tiptoes, his ass clenching. It was beautiful.

"See? A little color, and somehow he's even better." Packer moved her hand out of the way for a moment and gave Adrian a smack. Adrian gasped and Calleigh groaned softly, eyes on the handprint he'd left behind. "He loves it, huh?" Packer hit one more time, watching Adrian sway.

"Let me try?"

Adrian cried out, the sound strangled.

"Oh, yes." He backed off, letting Calleigh get into position.

She swung her hand back and the sound when she connected... Crikey, the sheila had some strength in her.

Adrian shouted, his whole body swaying, his arms giving out a moment. Packer went to him and helped him back up, positioning him so that sweet ass stuck out more.

"I'll take this side, huh?"

She met his eyes. "He's good?"

"He's good. Aren't you, Adrian?"

Adrian moaned, his ass moving side to side, begging for more.

She nodded, then took another swing, that hand landing again, hard.

Packer joined in, hitting the other cheek. In seconds they had Adrian dancing, ass moving, constant sounds pouring out of the man's mouth. That fine ass glowed, bright, dark red, the skin hot as hell. Packer waited until the tone of Adrian's cries turned desperate before he stopped, putting his hand over Adrian's skin. "Burning up."

Calleigh ran her nails over the skin. "Perfect, needy boy."

Adrian pushed back, legs spread, balls swaying. "Please."

Calleigh scratched that pretty ass, eyes twinkling. "Packer?"

"What do you want, luv? Want me to do him while he uses his mouth on you? You want to touch him while he sucks me? He'd let you."

"I want his mouth. I want to watch you fuck him. Hard."

How had Adrian left this girl home to wait?

Adrian glanced up and over one shoulder, eyes wet, face glowing. "Oh, God."

"You want us, Ades?" Her fingers stroked his hole, almost delicate.

Adrian's back arched, and by God he was the prettiest thing. "Yes. Fuck."

Calleigh leaned down, lips brushing the small of his back before she slipped around the side of the bed, unbuttoned her jeans. Packer moved up and rubbed his clothed body against Adrian's glowing backside.

"Fuck. Fuck." Adrian pushed back against him. Sweet little wanton. Needy.

"Mmmhmm. Look at your woman, Adrian. She's going to taste so good."

Their pretty Calleigh blushed, the tight jeans down, leaving her in the tank and tiny lace panties.

Packer rocked, his hand squeezing Adrian's hip. "So pretty."

Adrian grunted, nodded. "Too many clothes, baby. Want."

The little shirt disappeared, then the panties, and fuck, Packer could smell how she wanted them. He almost envied Adrian. Almost. He'd get to see everything, though. Everything. And he got that amazing, tight, burning ass.

When Calleigh slipped into bed and pushed herself up on the pillows, Packer moved Adrian by pushing on that hot bottom. "Between her legs."

Calleigh's fingers were sliding over her breasts, down her belly, over her thighs, and Adrian whimpered as he moved into place.

"Sweet." Laughing, Packer unbuckled his jeans. This was gonna be fun.

Calleigh grinned up at him, stared him up and down, and licked her lips. Packer hooted, pushing Adrian down when he would have looked back.

"Need you, Ades. I want your mouth," Calleigh said.

Adrian blinked over at Calleigh and his back moved with a deep breath. "Yes, baby girl. Want to taste you."

Packer could see Calleigh's belly go tight, hear the needy little gasp. Grinning, he pushed Adrian down again, and his chook went obediently, kissing Calleigh's belly and thighs. That gave him a great view — red ass, hard nipples, that dangling belly ring, Adrian's broad shoulders.

"God almighty." Packer cast about for the lube and all, not really wanting to move.

"Mmmhmm…" Calleigh's fingers were in Adrian's hair,

moving him. Adrian bent to his task with enthusiasm, these amazing noises coming from him, that hot ass rocking back and forth, up and down.

Packer finally broke and went to get the lube, needing Adrian now.

"Ades... Oh, fuck."

He glanced back, watching that amazing girl tugging her nipples, rocking up into Adrian's mouth. His cock pushed up harder toward his belly, and he moved back in behind Adrian, smiling down at Calleigh. "Ready?"

"God, yes. So ready."

"Good." He made short work of getting Adrian ready, only giving the man two wet fingers. He needed in, needed to hear Adrian cry out, needed to have Calleigh watch it. Packer covered and lubed up, pushing in behind Adrian, his cock at that tight hole.

Bright green eyes stared at him, and she smiled, the look slow and sensual, better than porn.

Gripping Adrian's ass, Packer shoved, getting past the initial resistance.

Adrian lifted his head, moaned, and Calleigh cried out, hips rolling.

"Going to fuck you so good, Chook."

"Please." Adrian's eyes turned to meet his. "Pack."

"Yeah, lover. I got you." Driving hard, he made his hips smack Adrian's ass.

Adrian grunted, wrapping around Calleigh to bring her closer. Her legs spread as her butt tilted, and he could see over Adrian's shoulder. Fuck, she was lovely. They all three found a rhythm, strong and steady. Adrian's ass burned around his dick, the lean hips fit right in his hands.

He stroked Adrian's back and listened to the insanely erotic sound Adrian's mouth made on Calleigh's flesh. Christ.

"Oh, fuck. Y'all." Calleigh was watching him, staring as his cock disappeared into Adrian's body.

Packer groaned, letting go with one hand to smack

Adrian's hip, reminding him how hot that ass was. Adrian grunted, ass squeezing him like a fist.

"Yes. Oh, you should feel him, love. He's so tight. Does his mouth feel good?"

"Uh-huh. Good. He's hungry." She rode Adrian's lips, belly tight.

"Yeah. Yeah, he is. Tight. Fucking hot."

"Good. Make him come on your cock," she moaned. Jesus Christ, listen to her.

"Gonna. I swear."

Adrian groaned, squeezing down around him, and whatever the hell he'd done to Calleigh made her cry out.

"Again! Ades, again."

Adrian rocked between them, like pure sex made into flesh. Packer swacked Adrian's hip again, knowing they were all right there, so close.

Adrian cried out, almost a roar, and bucked for them. Those hands on Calleigh's thighs tightened up, leaving red marks. Calleigh moaned out their names and slumped back against the headboard.

Packer took, oh, a second and a half to follow them, coming so hard he almost blacked out. Adrian was... Well, with Calleigh there, it was four or five times as good, not just twice.

They slumped together, making those amazing guttural, post-fuck noises. Packer grinned against Adrian's back, that ass on fire against his pelvis. Yum. He looked up, met Calleigh's eyes, and she winked. Once.

Yeah. Yeah, a man didn't have to win an event to have possibly the best night ever. He just had to have a really good ride.

Chapter Six

Calleigh leaned back in the water, soaking. Resting.

The boys were having a slump of mammoth proportion and she hadn't gone to today's event after they'd both snarled and growled this morning. Hell, between that and that goddamned Brandy bitch coming to rub all over Adrian for some bullshit photo shoot thing, she was more than a little grumpy herself. She knew about this part — lie low and be quiet. They'd played hard for five weeks, though, the boys flying ahead, her driving and following behind. They had two more events, then a two week break, and Calleigh hadn't thought about what she was supposed to do then.

She rubbed soap on her legs, shaving them while she tried not to think. She'd paid for the room tonight, not wanting to have to worry, but she thought maybe that made it worse.

Maybe they —

"...damn it, Chook. It's time for your sheila to go now. We can't keep doing this. We have to focus, mate. I can't keep this shit up. She needs to go home."

Calleigh winced, biting her lip as the razor slipped, nicking her leg. Fuck.

Okay.

Fuck. She pulled the plug and stood, grabbed her towel, and told herself to put it together. Time to go. Make a plan. A good plan.

She wrapped a towel around her hair, started putting on her makeup. Concealer. Base. Eyeliner.

"It's not like it's her fault, Pack." Adrian wasn't snarling, but he was standing up for her, which was dear.

"I ain't saying it is, but I'm worn out. One of us is gonna get hurt. She just needs to give us a few weeks."

She opened the bathroom door, smiled. "Hey, guys. Bathroom's free." She kissed Adrian's cheek, Packer's, then went to her laptop. Cruises came and went out of Charleston all the time. She needed to find one leaving in the next few days.

Packer went into the bathroom next, and Adrian wandered. A lot. He hung up a shirt and pulled out his riding jeans.

She found a cruise to the Bahamas, got herself a cabin, then pulled out Adrian's bags. "Y'all are flying out tonight, huh?"

"Yeah." He grinned halfheartedly. "Gotta go on to Memphis."

"Good deal. Let's get you ready." She had them packed before Packer was out of the bathroom, had herself wrapped in her robe.

Packer raised a brow at the laid-out clothes and the suitcases. He looked good naked and damp, muscled and scarred. His dark eyes didn't miss much, and his mouth curved into that crooked grin she was coming to love.

She forced herself not to respond, to keep her game face on. She needed them to go, soon, or she'd start crying, then all bets were off. "What time's the flight?"

"Nine-ish. We have time for some food, if you want." Packer really smiled for her now, that amazing face crinkling up.

"It's okay. I don't." She smiled back, holding her shit together. "I'm heading off. Taking a cruise, seeing the sights. Fun stuff." She grabbed her bag, tossed on a sundress, a pair of panties. "Call me after Little Rock, huh? Let me know if you want to hook up during your break."

Neither boy tended to ride the event in the Keys. It had been bad luck for them.

"Wait." Packer blocked her way. "What?"

"I'm taking a cruise. Y'all have a good one." She grabbed

74

her laptop, her toiletry bag, her phone, got everything in her purse while they stood there, staring at her. She kissed Adrian quickly, waved at Packer. "Good ride, y'all. Make money."

She could move like a whirlwind when she needed to.

Packer could move fast, too, but Adrian cut him off. "Have fun, baby girl. I love you." Adrian's voice was gentle. Knowing.

"I know." She winked, waved, and let the door close behind her. She didn't even cry a bit until she got to the truck in the parking lot, and by then she could let the storm come for a bit before she hit the road and went to explore.

"Okay, what the hell was that?" Packer slammed his hand against the door, right next to Adrian's head. Adrian was leaning on the door, blocking his way. "She just goes flat out like a lizard drinking, no telling us nothin'?"

Adrian nodded. "That's what you asked for, mate. That's what you got."

"I asked… I was blowing off steam. She couldn't have heard." Right? Calleigh had been in there with water running. Packer wasn't mad at her. He was frustrated at their lack of winning rides of late.

That made Adrian chuckle. "First thing, that woman has hearing like you can't imagine. She would've made one hell of a mom. Second, the best thing about Calleigh is also the worst. She hates being in the way, mate, and I told her once, wasn't nothing more important than the riding to me. She said she'd handle it. She does."

"I. Shit." Shit. He'd hurt her. Packer hadn't meant to, not at all. He'd been wanting to blame his slump on the nearest thing that wasn't him.

"No worries. We'll call her when we get done in Little Rock, see what she's up to."

He wasn't sure how Adrian could accept it, that she blew out like she blew in, so fast his head spun.

"No worries." Pack shook his head, backing off. "Shit."

"Yeah. You want anything to eat before we head for the airport?"

"No." His hands clenched and unclenched. He really wanted to beat something. Not Adrian, a heavy bag or something. He wasn't good at this relationship shit. "I'll get something there."

"Right." Adrian went to take his shower and he went to get his jeans. Calleigh'd packed damn near everything. Only thing she'd missed was one of his T-shirts she'd taken to tugging on at night so they had something to pull off.

Christ. Packer could smell her on it and he snarled a little, flinging the damned thing across the room. Before going to get it and stuff it in his carry-on. He might need it when they got to missing her.

Because, damn it. He was going to.

Chapter Seven

Calleigh headed into the hotel, checking her messages. The cruise had been fun — she'd laughed and danced, explored Nassau, and sunned herself judiciously. She'd gotten a massage, a facial and new highlights.

Calleigh was feeling good.

She checked her emails. Her texts. Adrian had sent her text updates, Packer was doing okay — had made money in an event, and Adrian was rocking, taking runner-up and winning yesterday's go-round. Packer'd sent one text, too.

It had been a wee bit more...graphic than Ades'. *"Miss fucking you,"* it had said.

Calleigh chuckled, going for the registration desk when Adrian's ring tone sounded and she frowned. He didn't call during events. Adrian always wanted to focus, to wait until after to talk to her.

"Hey, Ades."

"Hey, baby girl." Oh, no. Adrian sounded like hell. She knew every nuance of his voice, and this was not good, with a side order of 'eek'.

"What can I do?" She turned around, headed for the truck, trying to remember where they were riding.

"Pack is hurt, baby. I don't know how bad — they've taken him to the hospital already, and I got to ride yet."

"Okay. You're in...Shreveport?" She could be there in thirteen hours, twelve if she pushed it.

"Yeah. Yeah, it's kind of stinky here." Adrian laughed, and it sounded a little hysterical. "I don't even know the name of the hospital."

"I'll figure it. Hospitals I know. You get your mind on

the work. I'll be there as soon as I can." She hopped in the truck. "Love you, Ades."

"Love you, baby. I'm at the Sheraton. I'll have my cell and Pack's."

"All right. I'll call." She hung up, put Shreveport into the GPS and kept her eyes peeled for a Starbucks. Time to go to her boys.

* * * *

God, hospitals stank.

Packer was in surgery. Adrian had stuck it out through the night at the event, taking third in the round, but then he'd high-tailed it to the medical center. He needed to be there when Pack came out of it and woke up.

The coffee sucked hairy donkey balls.

"Hey, dude. How goes?" A huge Starbucks coffee was pushed into his hands, along with a bag of Burger King. Cotton was standing there, along with Fred and Kynan and Garrett. Some of his best friends in the whole league, thank fuck.

"Oh, hey, guys." Adrian smiled, blinking grit out of his eyes. "He's in surgery."

"Damn."

"Fuck."

"Fucking hell."

Fred sighed. "Is it bad, mate?" Fred was another Aussie, and he understood things the other guys didn't about visas and working and shit.

"His leg is all broken, I guess. Collarbone, too, so crutches will be a bear." So would Packer.

"Damn." Cotton was a little one-note sometimes, but he cared.

"He gonna have to stay here long?" Kynan asked.

"I don't know." The coffee hand started to shake a little, the food hand clenching in the bag.

"Okay. Okay, mate. You seem a little shell-shocked."

Fred eased him down into a chair. "You need us to call someone?"

"No. No, I called my wife. She's a nurse." He smiled. Dude. Fred knew that.

"Yeah, as in hello, nurse!"

He was going to kill Kynan.

"You leave my wife alone," Adrian mumbled, needing Kynan to back off.

Fred clapped him on the shoulder. "Here, let me open your food, huh? Cotton, pull up that little table."

"You got it, man."

He sat there and his phone rang. Calleigh.

"I'll be right back." He pushed past the guys, knowing his phone was supposed to be off. He headed to the nearest exit, pushing the answer button. "Hey, baby girl."

"Hey, you. I'm going to be there soon—an hour and a half, maybe less. How's it going?"

Shit, she must be flying down the road.

"Pack's in surgery. I'm not sure what kind of progress they're making." He bit his thumbnail.

"I'll be able to find out. Quit chewing on your nails. What have they said so far?"

"Doc said that he was shocky, and they had to wait to do the surgery until he was more stable. Then they told me they were taking him in."

"Okay, Ades. Hold it together. I'm going to be there. I can stay with him when you have to move on."

"I'm trying, baby. The guys brought me food." He just... God, he wanted to know that Pack was okay and have Calleigh there.

"Good deal. Go eat, talk to them. I'll be there before you know it." Solid as a rock, his Calleigh.

"Love you, baby. Glad you're on my side."

"Always." She meant it, too, damn it.

"I know. See you soon." He waited for her to hang up first. Then his stomach growled. Maybe he should go eat what they'd brought. It might make him less hysterical. The boys would keep him company until his girl showed.

* * * *

Calleigh parked, grabbed her purse and headed in, moving at a fast walk. Adrian didn't do well in hospitals, at best. At worst, he freaked out. She might call this a worst case scenario.

She knew he was on the third floor, so she made her way up, taking the stairs two at a time. There was a small sea of cowboy hats in the waiting room, all tilted down to cover faces. Everyone but Adrian was asleep. Ades? He was chewing his thumbnail.

She headed over, nudged Adrian's toe with her foot. "Hey, Ades."

He jumped a bit, then grinned and stood, hugging her hard. "Hey, baby."

"Hey." She kissed his cheek. "So, what did they say?"

"He's in recovery, I guess. All they said was the surgery was successful." He seemed pooped, hard lines along his mouth.

"Good deal. You doing okay?"

"I guess, yeah." He held on a little longer. "You get through the drive okay?"

"You know it. I'm a stud." Her fingers found the small of his back, stroking in circles.

"You so are. Oh, I missed you." He kissed her neck, and she could feel the tension seeping out of him.

"Good." She kissed his temple. "Pretty boy." She needed to find the shift nurse, peek at Packer's chart.

"Mmm. I've been holding it together, baby. Promise." He grimaced. "I have to leave out at three tomorrow. Hell, Doc already went, did his thing and got on the road."

"I can stay and take care of things. I'm sure Dr. Madding wouldn't have left him if he wasn't in good hands." She put on a patently false Aussie accent. "No worries."

That made him laugh for her, his hands on her hips.

"Thank God. Packer is worse than me."

"Eh. I'm a pro." She lifted her face for a kiss.

Adrian gave it to her, lips warm and firm on hers.

"There you go, Ades. You're good." She cupped his cheek.

"I am. Or I will be."

"You will. You have a place to sleep tonight?"

"I do. Got a king. Was hoping you'd be here."

"I am. Let me check his status, figure out what to do, then we'll get some sleep."

"That sounds like heaven." He smiled, better already.

"Give me ten minutes, Ades." She headed to the nurses' station, grinned. "Hey. I'm checking on Packer Stephens."

"Are you related?" The nurse smiled, though, going for sympathetic.

"I'm his wife." It was patently untrue, but she could fake it like no one's business.

"Oh, good. I'm so glad you're here." There was nothing like the little woman in a hospital to get news.

"How's he doing?"

"He's stable. His surgery went really well, but he's gonna be laid up for a while. Let me see if I can get the doctor."

"Thank you." She waved Adrian over.

Adrian came to stand next to her. "All good?"

"Mmmhmm. They're getting me the doctor. Packer needs to see his wife soon, after all." She winked.

Adrian blinked, then laughed, the sound rusty as all get out. "You know it."

She squeezed his hand, then held on and waited, as patiently as she could.

"Mrs. Stephens?" The doctor was like most orthopedic guys she knew. Tall, a little Lurch-like, and smiling gently.

She nodded, smiled. "Calleigh Roberts. I kept my own name. How's he doing?" All true.

"Well, he's had a severe fracture, but no bone fragments or deposits made it into the bloodstream. His leg will take a while, but we didn't have to go with any kind of traction. His collarbone is fractured as well. These are the kinds of injuries I usually see in traffic collisions."

She nodded. "Those bulls are powerful. How many pins?"

"Two." The doctor's head tilted. "Are you in the medical profession?"

"I'm an RN, doctor." She smiled, held one hand out.

"Oh, that makes my job easier." He grinned and shook her hand. "I don't think he'll require a facility recovery, but he will need some physio."

"I worked for two years in a therapy facility. I can handle it."

"Then we can sit down before he's discharged and talk about what he'll need. You can see him in about a half hour."

"Excellent. Thank you so much. I'm here for the duration. If the nurses need me, just let me know." That was better than she'd feared, way easier to work with.

"I'll do that. The cafeteria is on the first floor, if you need some coffee." He left them, nodding at Adrian.

"Well, that's not too bad, Ades, huh?" She could help with rehab.

"I guess." He seemed a little shell-shocked. "What did all that mean, exactly?"

"His leg's broken, they put pins in. He'll hurt for a couple days, and I'll take him home. I've seen these a lot. He'll be up and taking steps day after tomorrow."

"That soon?" Adrian shook his head, seeming lighter somehow.

"You know it. They'll want him moving as soon as the pain's handled." She touched his cheek.

"Okay. You want something to eat?" Ades stuck his hands in his pockets like he was afraid to reach for her.

"I do. McDonald's was a long time ago."

"So was Burger King." Adrian finally put a hand on her waist. "Can we go somewhere not here?"

"If you can wait for forty-five minutes, yes. We'll see him, then go eat, then go to the hotel."

"Okay. Then let's go get a coffee, at least." He steered her out of the room, leaving the sleeping cowboys behind.

She twined her fingers with his, held on tight.

Adrian gripped her hand like she was a lifeline, and it was good to know she could be there. That he felt like he could count on her. They grabbed two cups of coffee, three muffins, and they found a seat in the back. "How did you do at the event, Ades?"

"Fair, I guess. I was eighth overall." He shrugged. "I meant to text, but you know..."

"I do." She squeezed his hand. "You're forgiven. You had a good couple of weeks?"

"I have." He gave her a wry grin. "We've been like monks, baby."

"Why, Ades? Y'all having troubles?" Had she fucked them up? She hadn't meant to, not at all.

"Nope. He felt guilty, I think. He didn't mean to run you off, baby."

She shrugged. "I know I wasn't exactly invited in."

"No, but it works." Adrian reached over to take her hand. "I'm glad you came. Before. I mean now, too, but before."

"I had to give us a chance, Adrian. I love you."

"I love you, too, baby." He sighed. "Being on the road gets consuming."

"I know. No guilt. I just... I want you." *Both of you.*

"Good." He squeezed her hand, smiled again. Every time he did he seemed happier. "You made an impression on Pack."

Yeah. The 'it's time to get rid of the sheila' impression. "Is that good?"

"Hell, yes. He didn't mean it, you know."

"Of course he did. I was in the way."

"No, baby." He stared into her eyes, serious as hell. "Pack vents a lot. You'll have to learn that about him. He had to come up with a reason why we were in a slump."

"Because you didn't stay on." The joke was old, and not very funny anymore, but it was all she had.

"Yeah. Sucks when you let go and fall off." He winked.

"God, I'm tired."

"Let's go see Pack, then, and take you to sleep. I can help."

"Okay, baby. You're always so good to me." He stood, drawing her to her feet and kissing her mouth.

"I love you." She held on a second. "Let's go see him." Then they'd hit a bed and crash. At least that was the plan. Hopefully Packer wouldn't be unhappy to see her. That might make things awkward.

* * * *

Packer looked like hell. They'd been able to see him for maybe five minutes, almost awake, before they'd been kicked out. Packer was moving to a private room tonight. Adrian and Calleigh had gone on to the hotel, and Adrian was glad for it. He was worn to the bone.

She brought one bag up, locked the door, and starting stripping down. "Come shower with me."

"That's the best idea I've heard in an age." Adrian climbed up off the bed, listening to his bones creak.

"I have lots of them." She'd been outside, her tan was amazing.

"You do." He went to her, sliding his arms around her waist. "God, you're lovely."

"Do you think so?" She blushed for him, such a girl.

"I do. I always have."

She was more confident now. More amazing than ever. Calleigh leaned up, her lips pressed against his, moving slowly as she gave him the kiss he'd been wanting for days.

Adrian moaned, shifting against her, his hands starting to move. He knew all of her hotspots, knew how to get her going fast. She whispered his name into his lips, her hands hot on his chest. Adrian kissed her with everything in him. He needed her so bad.

Her nipples dragged along his chest and her hands dug into his hips. God, she was hotter than a summer sidewalk. He loved how she fit against him, how his cock rubbed her soft belly, even through his jeans.

"I need you, Ades. It's been weeks." She took his hand, brought it to her soft, damp curls.

"I know, baby girl. I know." He pushed her toward the bed instead of the shower, helping her stretch out. Then he stripped down, needing to be naked with her. She was propped up on one elbow, watching him, and he could smell her — citrus and musk.

She was fucking beautiful. Curvy and strong with the smoothest skin.

Adrian loved how she'd fought for him, wanted him. Made a man a little... Well, it gave him a swelled head of sorts.

"Come here, Ades. Prove you missed me."

"Fuck, yeah." He went to her, stretching out on top of her. He needed her more than his next breath.

She wrapped one leg around his hip and her lips brushed his. He slid his hand down to her hip, curving around to her butt. So soft. She moaned for him, the sound deep and rich and needy.

"Pretty girl." He kissed her throat, the tops of her breasts.

"Mmm. All tan for you."

Tan and luscious, he thought. "You have a good vacation, baby?" The tan made her all but glow.

"Uh-huh. Would have been better with y'all, but it was good."

"Oh, how fun would that be? We should go to the beach," he said.

"Oh, I'd like that."

He brushed her nipple and she gasped. "Me, too. I'd love it." Her in a bikini. Packer would go nuts. Packer loved the beaches back in Oz, too.

"We can go for Christmas break. You and me and Pack."

"Sounds good, baby." He rubbed against her, his cock slipping between her thighs.

"Good. Not now. Now it's you and me."

"Just us." He kissed her jaw line, the spot under her ear.

"Mmmhmm. Just us." Soft and willing underneath him.

Adrian couldn't wait anymore. He had to be inside her. Just had to. Adrian pulled back, spreading her legs wider, settling in.

"Yes. Yes, Ades. Please." She was so wet that he slid right in, her walls clinging to his cock.

"Baby." He stopped a moment, trying to breathe. "Oh, God."

"Mmmhmm." Her hips moved, body slamming down on his dick.

"Calleigh." God, he loved being inside her. She felt like nothing else, ever. Like a lock to his key, which was a cliché, but there it was.

"Love you." Her lips were against his ear, against his jaw.

"Yes. Oh. Yeah." Adrian moved faster, his hips rolling, his ass clenched hard to get good thrust.

Her hands were all over him like a cheap suit, nails digging in a little, scraping over his skin. Adrian shifted to get a better angle before moving faster, driving them higher and higher.

"Oh, Jesus. Ades!" Her hand slipped between them, fingers rubbing her clit but good.

"Come on, baby. I've got to— We have to hurry."

"Uh-huh." He felt her, clenching around him, jerking on his dick.

Oh, thank God. His balls drew up and his eyes rolled and Adrian poured maybe three days of tension right into Calleigh's body. She hummed for him, held him as he slumped down on her.

"Thank you, baby girl." He nuzzled at her neck, licking salt from her skin.

"Love you." She held on tight.

"Yes." They needed a shower, and they probably needed to talk. He was so tired, though, and she was so warm and perfect.

"Sleep, Ades. Rest a little."

"Stay with me?" He knew she should get back to Pack,

but he had to leave soon.

"I promise."

"Thanks, baby." Adrian settled in even better, his breath deepening, his eyes dropping closed. Right before he fell asleep—a good, deep sleep for the first time in days—he felt her lips on his temple, easing him down.

* * * *

Calleigh had left Adrian still sleeping hard at six a.m. and headed to the hospital, wearing a pair of jeans and a comfy T-shirt, something she could help out in. They'd be wanting Packer up and moving today, using the toilet, all that good stuff. She figured he'd hate having her help, but a friendly face was better than a stranger.

The wing Packer was in was still quiet, the nurses on duty telling her that visiting hours weren't open yet. Now, it was amazing what happened when she told them she was an RN. She slid into his room, careful not to wake him, and checked his vitals.

Bless his heart, he was one giant bruise. The collarbone was going to be a bitch. Ultimately it would be worse than the leg, considering what he did for a living.

She took his blood pressure as carefully as she could, recording the numbers. Not bad.

Those long eyelashes fluttered, Packer's lips moving.

"Shh. You're okay, Pack. I've got you."

"Cal..." He swallowed and tried again. "Calleigh?"

Well, that was a fabulous sign. He knew who she was, and considering how little time they'd spent together, that meant he was fairly aware.

"That's right, lover. Ades called and I came running." Ridiculous, but true.

He blinked, his eyes dark as night. "Calleigh? It really is you, huh, luv?"

"It is. How're you doing?" She leaned down, kissed his cheek.

"Fair, I reckon." He grinned, enough to pull his mouth. "You look good."

"Thank you. You look like hammered shit." She winked, got the glass of water from his bedside table and held the straw to his mouth.

He drank enough to get everything wet, not enough to make him sick. She got the feeling he'd been down this road before. "Adrian? He all right? Did he ride?"

"Yeah, yeah, he did. He did good. Eighth overall."

"Good on him." Packer swallowed again, like he was testing his lips and tongue. "How'm I doing?"

"Not bad. Two pins. Leg looks good. Clavicle's going to take longer to heal than that."

"Yeah." He grimaced. "This bed is for shit."

"I've got the truck. I'll be able to take you home in a couple days." She figured she could stay at Packer's, at least until Adrian got back on a long break, surely, and if he needed his space sooner, she'd step back and punt.

Selling the house hadn't been her smartest decision, but at the time, she'd figured she'd never ever need it again.

"Yeah?" He cracked another smile. "All that time alone with me. Whatever will we do?"

"I'm betting one of us sleeps a lot and knits his bones." She winked at him, smoothed the hair off his forehead.

"Yeah." His eyelids drooped, slurring.

"Shh. Sleep. I got your vitals. You'll get another pain pill in an hour or so."

"When can I have a cigarette?" He was trying valiantly, but he was fading back into sleep.

Calleigh chuckled, patted his hand. "Soon."

"'Kay. Thanks, luv. For coming. Din' mean it." Then he was asleep, his body relaxing a little.

As soon as he was good and out, Calleigh got her stuff together. Time to get one more snuggle in with her Ades before they both came back up.

Chapter Eight

"Fucking hell." Packer lay on the floor like an overturned turtle, completely unable to push himself up now that he was down. The leg was bad enough, but the collarbone was evil incarnate.

God damn, he was tired of sleeping in the big chair in the lounge instead of bed. He was tired of Adrian being a voice on the phone, and he was fucking tired of Calleigh acting like all she was to him was a bloody nursemaid and someone to answer his sometime-foreman Rob's fucking questions. Hell, Calleigh was sleeping on the fucking couch in the front room like she was a stranger. It made no fucking sense.

"Are you down there on purpose or would you like to get up?" She'd put up with him screaming at her for every bump the entire drive down—she'd fed him, bathed him. Now she was staring at him like he was a fool.

Maybe he was.

"No, I think I'll stay down here. Can't manage to walk."

She chuckled softly, then knelt down next to him. "You'll get cold."

"I will. I'll atrophy, too." He'd waste away, and that would be sad.

"Not on my watch." One hand slid down his arm, the touch so fucking good. "Come on. I'll help you get up and I'll feed you. I made chili."

"Yeah?" He liked her cooking so far. She'd made a lot of soup, but hardly ever the same kind twice. He loved the chicken tortilla stuff, all spicy and tomato and cheese.

"Yep. Cornbread, too." She wore sweats and tank tops a

lot. He'd seen her in jeans and boots, too, out checking the cattle, like he needed someone to do that. He had a guy living in a trailer in the acreage by the road that rode fence, fed, all that shit. She cowboyed up pretty good.

"I like your cornbread." Her cornbread was actually a revelation. She made it in cast iron, and it got crunchy bits on the outside... Heaven. He was starting to see the benefits of Texas, beyond the land thing.

"I know." Her hands kept moving on him, letting him feel something good.

"Well, I reckon I should get up." She was strong as anything, too. She'd get him upright.

"Okay, then, come on." She knew how to do it, to get him up and stable.

They got him to his feet, and he only bellowed once. Then he was back in his fucking chair, his leg up, all his pillows arranged. He was going to go insane.

"Your face is going to stick like that." She got him his remote, a TV tray, then brought chili and milk and cornbread for him.

"It can't be much worse, luv." Packer sighed. "Sorry. I know I'm bad company."

"No biggie. In my line of work, most people are grumpy." She pulled her bright red hair back into a ponytail. "Holler if you need me — I'm going to clean up the kitchen."

"I'm not a job." He snarled it at her, and he was sorry for it, really. But he needed to say it.

Her eyes went wide, and he could see the hurt for a half second, then it was gone. "No, you're not."

Packer reached for her with his good hand, grabbing her wrist when she tried to turn away. "Sorry, luv. I really am. Did I tell you I didn't mean it? What you heard in the hotel? I was blowing off steam."

She nodded, but her eyes didn't meet his. "I know. It's okay. It's a lot, to have somebody extra around all the time."

"Extra?" He shook his head, which sent his collarbone to twinging. "Luv, you're Adrian's wife. That's not the same."

She did look at him this time. "No, it's not, but it's still the truth. At least over the last few years, y'all were the couple. I get it. I wasn't sure you'd let me tag along and play. I was tickled you did."

"Tag along..." God. He was a right bastard, if that was how she felt. "I thought it was pretty clear how much I liked you along."

"You were. We had fun. If you ever let that collarbone heal, hopefully we can do it again." She squeezed his hand, then pulled away. "You need to eat before that chili gets cold. I didn't make enough for extra this time."

"Okay." Damn it, he was tired. He wanted to argue with her some more, but he didn't have the energy to do it.

She kissed his temple, her lips warm, soft.

Oh, that was far better. Packer grinned. "Now that I like."

Calleigh chuckled for him, her breast warm and soft against his shoulder. "Horndog."

"I am. I can't help it." He yawned hugely, his jaw popping. "A tired one."

"Well, turkey. Eat. Then you can take your pills and rest."

"'Kay. I— Thank you, Calleigh. I know you don't have to be here." He wanted her to know that it meant a lot to him.

"Sure I do." She smiled at him, then headed out—to do dishes, then get on the damnable treadmill again, he'd bet. He heard it all hours of the day and night. She was in his workout room all the damned time.

Adrian's ring tone sounded and he grabbed his phone.

"Mate! You sound better!" Adrian said.

"I'm fucking miserable and don't you forget it, Chook." It was so good to hear Adrian's voice.

"Is our girl being mean to you?"

"No. No, she's not. She's not being all that nice, though." She wouldn't spend any time with him. She avoided him. It was making him crazed.

Adrian's laughter surprised him a little. "Ah. Nurse Calleigh. She's a tough broad, that one, but it's nice to be able to snarl at her and not have her burst into tears."

"Well, yeah. I hate to eat alone, though." Not to mention the fact that his one arm didn't work.

"You asked her to come sit, then? Because she's sounding a little lost when I talk to her."

"No. I didn't think she wanted to." Okay, half the time he couldn't stay awake once she fed him.

"Ah. Well, you might. Or not. Whatever, mate. Miss having you about, though."

All of a sudden he missed Adrian with a seriousness that made him ache. "Miss you, too, Chook. Really."

"I know."

He barely caught sight of Calleigh, her ponytail bobbing as she disappeared. There were his pills in a little juice glass, waiting for him.

Packer blinked. Damn. She didn't have to run off. "You want to talk to Adrian, love?"

"It's okay. He'll call."

"She's making me crazy. Shoot me. I can't jack off, I can't work out…"

"Get Calleigh to help you, Pack. She's got great hands." Adrian's voice lowered. "I'd help, if I was there."

Oh. His body made a valiant attempt to come to attention. "I know. I do. Soon, yeah?"

"Two weeks and I'm home for ten days. Calleigh says you'll be in your own bed way before then."

"I hope so. The chair is old. Not as bad as the hospital, though."

"Eh, you should be here. This hotel is so nasty that Calleigh'd be sleeping in the truck."

"Better or worse than the van?" The old van they used to travel in was always the gold standard of ew.

"Worse. It smells like Hank's socks."

"Oh, you poor baby. How is Hank?"

"Good. He's riding second right now. Joa's on top at the moment."

"No shit?" Wow. Joa was good, but there was always someone who came out above him.

"For now, yeah." Adrian sighed. "The guys want pizza again."

Adrian got tired of the weird-assed pizza Cotton and Garrick and Kynan dared each other to eat.

"So go have a burger. See if you can find that Landon kid." Adrian liked Landon, weird little Cajun that he was.

"Yeah. Yeah, maybe. What do you have?"

"Chili and cornbread." He knew Adrian would be jealous.

"No way! She's cooking for you?"

"Yep. Is that good?" He knew it tasted good, but he wasn't sure if it was a good sign.

"God, yes. Otherwise you get canned."

"Oh." He wondered how he could get fired in this situation, then he realized Adrian meant tinned food. "Oh! Well, good on me, then."

"You know it." Adrian sighed for him. "Talk to her a little, huh? She wants to get to know you."

"Okay, Chook. I'll be good." He would try. Sometimes he wasn't good at good. He was a right grumpy bastard.

"Now, mate. I didn't say that..."

He laughed, knowing how Adrian would want him to be very bad. "I'll see you soon, huh?"

"Yeah, mate. Take care."

"I will. Ride good."

They hung up, and he heard Calleigh's cell ring.

"Hey, Ades. Huh? No. No, I'm trying to be helpful, but I think he'll be happier when you're back. Hmm? Running a lot. Cooking some." Her voice trailed off. She had closed herself in the workout room, and Packer didn't figure he ought to intrude. She'd let him be, after all.

Something was going to have to give, though. Packer had a bad feeling that it was going to be his sanity.

* * * *

Packer had the most uncomfortable, evil couch on earth in his front room—it was huge, overstuffed, leather, and completely wrong for sleeping on. Calliegh'd been on it nine days, and she'd finally figured out, if she slept with all her upper body curled on the arm, she could manage.

It was a weird situation—Packer missed Adrian so much, and she spent a lot of time wondering if maybe she'd made a mistake, trying to be with Packer, too, because she could have feelings for him and he put up with her because she was Adrian's wife and maybe she wasn't good at that either, because Adrian had been doing fine without her and...

She sighed and checked the clock. Three a.m.

Go. To. Sleep.

This sort of thing took time, right? Right. There wasn't a textbook and there wasn't a support system and if she wanted them, then, damn it, she was going to have to work it out.

After she slept.

For fuck's sake, she had to give Pack's foreman money for feed and run for groceries and see if someone in town could fix the front step of the ranch house.

About twenty to four she got up, took a Valium with a glass of orange juice, and soon she was sound asleep. When she woke up, the sun was shining and her left boob was stuck to the couch. And Packer was staring at her.

"I. Hey." She blinked, trying to get her shit together. "Mornin'."

"Why are you on the couch?" He sounded grumpy.

"I was sleeping."

"I know that, woman. What I don't know is why."

She sat up, straightened her tank top, and tried to unfuddle herself. "It was nighttime. Jesus, I need coffee. You want a cup?"

"I'll take some, yeah." He was standing. Not too steady, but up on his own. "I mean, why weren't you in the bed?"

"Huh? There's only the one." Besides, he hadn't offered and the guest bedrooms were filled with boxes of stuff, mostly Adrian's. She grabbed a pair of shorts from her suitcase, pushed it back behind the big chair.

"Uh-huh." He raised one dark brow. "It's not gross or anything. Why aren't you...? Christ. Is that your suitcase?" He was glaring full-on now.

"Yeah..." She tugged her shorts on, trying to figure out what the fuck she'd done wrong.

"There's room for your shit in the closet!" He grimaced, like the shouting had hurt him.

"I'm sorry." She wasn't sure why he was so pissed off — her suitcase wasn't in anyone's way. "I'll put it away in a second."

Jesus. She headed for the kitchen, trying to keep her shit together, trying not to have a meltdown.

"Calleigh," he called to her, and she could hear the thump of his big cast on the floor. "Damn it, would you come back here?"

She took a deep breath, counted to five, then turned and headed back, catching him by the waist as he tottered. "I've got you."

His good hand landed on her shoulder. "You shouldn't feel like you aren't welcome here, luv."

"I just..." She didn't know what to do and she didn't know how not to fuck things up. "I'm just trying to help out, make things easier."

"You are. Helping. But you're not some hired wench, love. You need to be comfortable, too." He sighed, shook his head. "Can we sit?"

"Okay. Sure." She led him to his chair, frowning when he shook his head. "The couch wasn't as comfy for you..."

"Well, then come on and let's go sit in the bedroom." He stared at the chair a moment. "I'm getting a real hate-on for the chair."

"I bet." She let her hand slide across his lower back, massaging some. It felt so good for her to touch him in some way that wasn't impersonal and nurse-like.

He led her into the bedroom and she got him settled, got pillows propped around him. Then he held out his good hand and yanked her down when she took it. He grunted with what sounded like satisfaction.

She didn't know what to say, so she didn't say anything. Truthfully, she could lie down right here and sleep.

Packer yawned hugely, so big she heard his jaw pop. "C'mere, luv." He pulled her close enough to give her a kiss.

"Oh." She wanted to cuddle in, to rest for a while. She was so fucking tired.

"Mmmhmm. Feels so good." Packer sounded happy, a touch fuzzy.

"Not hurting you?"

"Not a bit." He yawned again, making it a long, drawn-out sound. "We should talk."

"What about?" If he told her to leave now, she'd bite him.

"I dunno. You seemed so upset."

Wait. She'd been upset? Men. "You're the one rumbling and growling."

"You slept on the couch." Packer said it like it was perfectly reasonable, like it made sense that he was upset by that.

"I didn't think you'd mind." What, she was supposed to sleep on the floor?

"I don't mind, luv. I can't believe you didn't sleep in the bed. You're not some unwanted guest."

"It's your bed, Pack. It seemed rude, to just take it." She glanced at him and bit her bottom lip hard so she wouldn't cry. "I've never done this before. I know you didn't ask for me. I know that I showed up, but..." She shrugged. She'd been lonely and bored and wanting her lover. She hadn't really believed Adrian would say yes, and she sure hadn't believed that she'd start feeling things for Packer.

"Shh." He tugged her up and kissed her again. "Hush, luv. You're all right. I promise. You're welcome to the bed and the closet, yeah?"

"Okay." She was so tired, bone deep. Now. "I'm sorry." She wasn't even sure what for.

"Calleigh. Don't be daft." He pulled her right up to his

side, yawning one more time.

"Not. Just... I'm tired." She surprised herself by tearing up, taking a hitching breath.

"Shh. I know, love. I do" He patted her clumsily.

She kissed his shoulder, eyelids too heavy to keep open. Valium. Damn Valium.

"Sleep now, luv. We'll figure this, now I know what the problem is." Packer sounded so sure. Confident.

Her hand rested on his belly and, oh. Oh, he was warm and cozy and close and right there. Close. Perfect.

* * * *

Packer woke up stiff as a board, but somehow feeling better than he had in days. He realized pretty quick that he wasn't in the blasted chair, he was propped up in bed with a sleeping woman next to him. Calleigh. Damn, he hoped she'd gotten some sleep.

He thought maybe she had. The huge dark circles were gone, the lines around her mouth had faded and she was smiling, even in her sleep. That was so pretty, that little smile. Packer wondered if she was dreaming of Adrian.

He reached out, touched her bottom lip, and Calleigh hummed. "Pack..."

Oh. Damn. She knew. She knew who she was with. If he could get over where he could kiss her, he sure would. "Calleigh. Luv. Come and kiss me."

Her eyes blinked open and her smiled widened. "Mmm. I was dreaming about you." She leaned up, warm and soft against him, as she offered him her lips, and Packer kissed her, the taste of her delicious.

Damn, she was fine, lazy and curvy and close. His leg was barely hurting, his collarbone only throbbing a little. If he was lucky, he could figure out a way to make them both happy. Surely a nice orgasm or two would remind her that he wanted her here, too.

The logistics were a bit daunting, but he was willing.

He'd figure it out.

She leaned back, then stretched, the tank top sliding to bare her nipples. "Are you hungry?"

"Mmmhmm." He slid his good hand up and down her back, encouraging her to move, to straddle his thighs. "A little horny."

"You are feeling better." Those pretty nipples started getting stiff for him.

"Mmmhmm. Maybe not good enough for a full-on tumble, but I like it when you touch me, luv." He liked a lot about her. There was a goodly bit of touching going on, too. He could feel her, hot and wet, through two layers of fabric.

He touched where he could reach without stretching too much, but he had to admit it was fun. Letting her do the doing.

"Tell me if I hurt you. I don't want to." Her fingertips slipped over his belly.

"No. No, we're good." He hoped they were, anyway. He knew one misstep could be bad.

"I'll be careful." She angled off him, hand on his dick, moving on him.

Packer moaned. It was so nice to feel something good. Something that didn't hurt. Calleigh's hands were strong — it still fucking surprised him, how strong she was. He didn't push up with his hips, even if he wanted to. He knew better. Lord, that time Adrian had broken a rib and tried to let Packer tie him to the bed…

Her thumb pushed over the slit of his cock, digging in enough to sting.

That made him grunt, made sweat pop up on his forehead. "Calleigh…"

"Uh-huh?" She met his eyes, pure evil.

"I need." He needed her skin and her smell and to be able to goddamn move.

"I've got you. You're okay." She leaned down, lips sliding over the tip of his dick, her hair pooling in his lap.

He was so okay. That felt like heaven. Her mouth was

fever-hot, her hair cool and silky. How the fuck had he found two people who loved to suck, who had mouths like this? He was a lucky, lucky man. Packer watched Calleigh, watched her move on him, making these crazy noises.

She stroked his balls, nudged them.

"Fuck!" His belly drew in, his hips trying to rise.

She pressed him down, heavy on him, keeping him still.

"Jesus, woman. Gonna kill me." He was panting, his cock aching.

Her laughter tickled all the way along his fucking dick. Packer laughed for sheer joy. What else could he do? She tickled behind his balls, scratched a little.

He gritted his teeth, his head falling back. One, two, three... That was it. Boom.

She took him in, tongue gentle on him, cleaning him off.

His body flopped down like a landed fish. "Calleigh."

"Mmmhmm..." She kissed his inner thigh, then pulled away. "Better?"

He wasn't sure that was the word for it at all. Packer felt wrung out and euphoric. "What about you, luv?"

"I'll manage. You're hurt."

"I could watch." He was a man, wasn't he? Ever hopeful.

One of her eyebrows arched. "You and Adrian... Or is it all men that love to see that?"

"Oh, luv. Boys like to see that. You could ask one of the Four fucking Horsemen and they would admit they liked it."

She wrinkled her nose. "Not a sexy thought, Pack. Try harder."

"Oh." No, it wasn't sexy at all. Okay, foul. Packer laughed. "I like it, luv. I like it a lot. Adrian used to tell me how you did it for him once. Do you remember? When he fell off the bull forward and broke both arms?"

"God, yes. He was miserable." She wriggled around so he could see her, but they were still touching.

"Mmm. He tells me about it a lot, in fact." Packer remembered the first time Adrian had pulled that story out.

It had nearly set them ablaze. They'd fucked like madmen.

"Really?" She met his eyes, suddenly vulnerable as all hell.

"Yeah, luv." Packer pushed a bit of her hair back with his good hand. "He talks on you a lot. Misses you." It was the truth.

Her blush stained her cheeks right up, and he'd be damned if her lip didn't quiver for half a second. She hid it pretty well, though, turning to nuzzle his hand.

Packer let her hide for a bit before pulling her to him for a kiss. "I can see why, now. Huh?"

"Good. I want you to." Oh, there was their fierce little sheila again.

"Yeah?" He smiled, starting to get a little blinky, sleepy. "Well, okay, then."

She chuckled, kissed his nose. "Nap. I'm going to jump in the shower and get some stuff done."

Packer tried to argue, but settled on, "If you, you know, in the shower. You have to tell me about it."

"You'll have to guess." She winked, playful, teasing.

"I'll know," he said. She was so much more comfortable now, he thought.

"Maybe." She slipped away from him, her little tank top tugged down to cover her ass, those amazing legs.

"Don't stay gone forever, luv." The last word slurred. He could sleep now. The last thing he heard was the shower in the master bath coming on.

* * * *

She finished her fifth mile of the day, then she hit stop on the treadmill, panting hard. Fuck, that never got easier. She headed to the kitchen, breathing deep, hunting a glass of tea. The phone rang while she was rummaging in the fridge. Her phone.

"'Lo?" She panted the word out, sweat dripping.

"Hey, baby girl. Have you been running?" Adrian

sounded tired.

"I have. How're you, Ades?"

"Good. Riding hard. How are you, baby?"

"Sweaty." She chuckled softly. "I probably need to check on Pack here in a minute and shower." She actually felt better than she had in days, after her nap this morning.

"Mmm. Sweaty." He laughed a little. "I like that."

"Are you okay? Just lonely?"

"Yeah. Yeah, I'm okay. Riding good, actually. I sent a check yesterday."

"You're a good man." She poured a big glass of tea. "Miss you."

"I miss you, too, baby. The guys have been great, but I would love to have your smiling face." Adrian lowered his voice. "And your boobs."

She chuckled softly. "They're in desperate need of attention."

"Are they? Poor Pack. That broken collarbone must be cramping his style."

"Yeah. I wasn't sure that he even wanted me here, but... Maybe he does, yeah?" She wanted to believe that. She was starting to.

"Of course he does, baby." Adrian chuckled. "He keeps asking me what to do to make you more comfortable."

"Yeah? I need a long bubble bath, shave my legs."

"Sleep with him at night, huh? He hates to sleep alone."

So did Adrian. He must be miserable. "I will." She chuckled, leaned against the counter. "I need to find a safe place to hide my vibrator."

"If Chook was here I could give you a fabulous place for it." Packer hobbled in from the front room, grinning like a fool.

She squeaked and jumped, damn near dropping her phone. "Shit. Oh, God."

She and Adrian and Packer all cracked up. Packer leaned against the counter and laughed, and oh, that lit up his hard face. Made him so hot. She found herself watching, her whole body on high alert, a soft moan sounding.

"Baby?" Adrian was talking through laughter. "You still there?"

"Uh-huh. Yeah. Yeah, I am. Wanna say hi to Pack?"

"Nah. I'll call him later. You get him to show you the best place to hide that vibrator, okay?"

"Ades!" She cackled.

"Love you, baby. I'll get a break soon."

"I can't wait, Ades. We'll be here."

"Okay. Give Pack a hug for me."

"I will." She said their goodbyes, then hung up, gave Packer a grin. "You doing okay?"

"I am." He was still grinning hard. "How's Adrian?"

"Lonely. He wants to come home. Here. Whatever." Well, that was weird.

Packer nodded, his dark eyes serious, watching her. "Is it weird, luv? Not having your house?"

"Sometimes. I mean, I have a storage building with special stuff, but…" She shrugged, suddenly a little sad. "I thought for sure Ades would say no and I knew I couldn't go back, so…"

"Oh, luv, you shouldn't have to pay for a storage thing. Bring it all here."

She blinked up, surprised. "Really?"

"Yeah." He nodded, then grimaced a little. "Fucking collarbone. The leg is barely there, you know?"

"Yeah, I know. That scapula break is a bitch." She wandered over to him, leaned up for a careful kiss. "I'm sweaty or I'd hug you. You want some tea?"

"Sure, luv." He raised a brow. "Getting sweaty without me?"

"Running. More than five miles today." She went to get Packer a glass.

"Christ." When she glanced over her shoulder he was smiling, not angry-looking at all. "That's a lot of running."

"I have to work to keep that last layer of hip and belly off." Hell, she'd worked viciously hard to make her body something people would notice.

"Yeah." Packer patted his belly. "I'll be flabby time I can do crunches again."

"You don't have an ounce of flab on you." She brought him his tea.

"You like?" His abs contracted, showing off his cut belly, which was as good as any calendar shot of firemen or whatever.

She licked her lips, fingers trailing over the muscles. "Mmmhmm."

His muscles quivered for her, which was gratifying, as she knew he wasn't ticklish. Adrian had told her. So it had to be her.

Jesus, she was horny. She let herself touch a bit more before she pulled back. "I need a bath." Her voice was all husky.

"Can I help?" Packer perked right up, standing and thumping over to her.

"Me shave my legs?" She pinked, grinned.

"You have no idea what a thing that is." He winked.

"No, but you can come watch." She grabbed their teas, letting her hips sway side to side.

"I'm all over that." Packer followed with gratifying speed.

"Are you going to be comfortable on the toilet?" She stripped off her tank top, turned the water on.

"I'll be fine, love." His fingers trailed down her spine.

She arched, she couldn't help it. Those callused fingers felt so good.

"Such soft skin." His accent was way heavier than Adrian's, and it was sexy as hell. He traced her ink, the touch making her hips rock. "So you like bubbles?" he asked.

"I love bubbles. Do you have bubble bath?"

"Uh-huh. Under the sink." His fingers traced the line of her hip.

"Oh, you rock…" She bent, trying not to blush too much as she gave Pack a show.

Pack moaned, the sound rough and genuine, and she felt better all of a sudden.

She found the bubble bath, grabbed it. *Oh, strawberry. Yum.* She poured a generous amount in, laughing as the bubbles started to form.

"Smells good, huh?" she asked when he hummed for her. She'd almost forgotten he was there. Almost.

"It does. Smells like one of those Slushie things. I always liked those."

"Next time I go get gas, I'll bring you home one." She slipped into the water, moaning at the heat. "Oh, God."

Packer shifted on the pot, watching her. "I'd like that."

"Cherry or Coke flavored?" She stretched out, legs sliding together. Oh. Oh, that was nice.

"Cherry, luv. I like the fruity." Packer blinked, then laughed.

"Uh-huh. I heard that about you." She chuckled, muscles melted, toes wiggling. He did have a happy laugh.

"Imagine that. So what do you wash first, love?"

"Mmm?" She lifted one leg out, rubbing the bubbles in. She'd never really thought about it.

"Legs, then." Packer shifted again like he couldn't get comfy.

She sat up, a little worried. "You okay?"

"I'm enjoying the show, luv." Packer glanced down at the zipper of his jeans, which he wore with one leg cut all the way to his thigh.

"Oh."

Of course, then his eyes landed on her — on her breasts, with the suds and bubbles dripping off her hard nipples.

"Uh-huh. Wish I could come in, but there's this damned thing. Don't stop, though."

"No. I won't." She sank back into the water, hands sliding along her legs again. The water felt so good.

Pack's eyes on her felt better. He watched her every move like she was the most tantalizing thing on earth, licking his lips occasionally. She touched up her legs with the razor, thankful there wasn't much, because hotness aside, Sasquatch legs weren't sexy.

Packer hummed a tuneless little song.

Calleigh closed her eyes, pretended that she was home, wanting, that she was alone and slick and naked. That was the only way she could do it and not feel silly. Really.

Until Packer started talking. "I told you Adrian used to tell me about this, yeah? About when he broke his arms?"

She nodded. "He was miserable and he couldn't touch. I sucked him a lot, spent a lot of personal time with my vibrator."

"Mmm. He told me about how he snuck in and watched you in the shower. You had a massaging shower head."

Her eyes flew open. "He told you that?" She blushed hot, bit her bottom lip. She'd been so hot she couldn't not.

"He did. In loving detail. He was very fond of the way you went up on tiptoes. Said it made your tits push up like heaven." Packer was grinning, hungry and feral, his hard face predatory as hell.

One of her hands slipped between her legs, the bubbles hiding the motion. "He is a breast man."

"He is. He loves yours. Says they're perfect for his hands."

It made her feel like a million dollars, knowing that Adrian talked about her, about wanting her. "What about you? Are you an ass man?" She winked over.

"I like all the parts." Packer chuckled, the sound like more warm water sliding over her. "I like your legs, luv. Your tits. I like your butt, too, but I admit that Adrian has you there."

She rolled her eyes, not offended in the least. Adrian had a fine ass, but if you were into male ones, hers most certainly wasn't. "Adrian's got a tight little tush."

"It's what he can do with it that's amazing." Packer arched a dark brow. "You stopped scrubbing."

"Did I?" She laughed and let one hand slide up over her belly, the other still gliding through her curls. She'd shave again for Adrian, when he got back.

"Mmm. Better." Packer reached down with his good hand, opening his fly.

Calleigh nodded, legs moving restlessly as her fingers slid lower, circled her clit. She could see Packer's nose twitch, could see his hips rolling. He was so damned responsive. The hand at her breast slid up, fingers starting to tease one of her nipples, tug hard enough that she felt it in her belly.

"God, luv. Look at you."

No. No, she'd rather look at him, so she did. He was pure sex, cock hard and dark, pushing out into his hand. Calleigh moaned, licked her lips and tugged again, her nipple aching so good.

Packer panted for her, his body moving as much as it could, restlessly.

"You..." God, she wanted to fuck. Her fingers worked harder, faster, her toes pushing on the bottom of the tub.

"So pretty. God damn, love. Adrian needs to come home so I can watch him fuck you."

She whimpered and nodded, her body sliding in the water. She was burning alive.

Packer's cast clunked against the sink cabinet when he lifted his hips to get his jeans down farther. "Calleigh."

"Want you, Pack." She pinched a little harder, rubbed a little faster, her body aching.

"Want you, too, love. So bad. Love to see you all wet and pretty like this."

She propped one leg up, bearing down on her fingers, the water sloshing.

"Oh, God. You. Please, luv. Need to see you come," he said, panting.

"Packer..." She dipped her chin, breath huffing out of her as she came, shaking and moving on her own hand.

A low moan was Packer's response, and she could smell him when he came, right there. For her.

She came down off her high, licking her lips, muscles loose and lazy.

Packer was slumped back against the tank of the toilet,

eyes crossed. "Whoa."

"Uh-huh." She rinsed off, sat up, water dripping off her.

Packer grinned at her, tired, but happy. "Adrian was right. I'm surprised the water's not boiling."

"Listen to you." God, that made her all tingly.

"It's the truth, luv." He tucked his cock back in his pants, patting it into place with a move so intrinsically male that it made her grin.

"Let me wash my hair and I'll help you get settled. You want to watch a movie tonight?"

"That sounds good. Do we have popcorn?" She noticed he didn't try to get up.

"We do. What movie?" She stood up, pulled the plug, then started the shower.

"Oh, I dunno. Nothing chick flick."

She leaned back into the spray, wetting her hair as she chuckled. "Spoilsport." She hated click flicks.

"Uh-huh. Adrian also told me about how much you love the Rocky movies."

"He's telling tales out of school." She soaped up, lather building between her fingers.

"Is he? So his favorite movie isn't *Groundhog Day*?" He laughed. "I know you, luv. I never got to meet you much."

"His favorite Bill Murray movie is *Groundhog Day*, but he's a secret *Tank Girl* lover."

"No shit?" That got her a raised brow. "Now that I didn't know. Sneaky monkey."

She chuckled and rinsed off. "Uh-huh. Me? I love monster movies—not serial killers or anything, but monsters."

"Then we should watch something monster. *Godzilla*."

"Yeah? You don't mind?" She rinsed off the rest of the soap, grabbed a towel.

"Not a bit. I love scary, rar." As soon as she dried off, he held up his good hand. "Easy on me, now."

She stood between his legs, bare naked, bending down to help him up.

"Thanks." He tottered a moment, leaning on her, then

straightened up. "I'm gonna hit the sofa."

"You want to…" She pinked. "You'd be more comfortable on your bed—we could watch in there." Cuddle, maybe.

"Oh." He brightened, that amazing smile right there. "Yeah. We could snuggle up."

"Yeah." She went up on tiptoe, kissed his jaw. "I'll get Cokes and popcorn. Well, after I grab a nightie."

"Oh, now. That's sad. A nightie." He winked, but let her ease him down on the bed and prop him up, his jaw only clenching a little.

"Be good or I'll steal a T-shirt. That makes Adrian crazy." She got the pillows settled around him.

"I have a—what do you call them? Tank top? You'd look ace in that."

"Is it soft?" He nodded and pointed and she dug one out. It was butter-soft and didn't leave anything to the imagination, but long enough that her butt was all covered, so it worked. The expression on Packer's face was worth it, too. He admired the look with a purely wolfish smile.

"I'll go grab our popcorn and drinks." She tossed him the remote.

"Thanks, luv. You're tops."

It was like the more he was away from cowboys, the more Aussie he became.

Her phone was blinking when she went back to the kitchen, Adrian's text showing up.

Miss U. Give P a show 4 me.

She popped the popcorn in the microwave, grabbed two Cokes and typed back—

Anytime, Ades.

Chapter Nine

Adrian was dragging ass. The flight had been delayed a thousand fucking hours and he'd gotten in at three a.m. He'd called Calleigh at nine and told her not to bother coming to get him—he would take a shuttle. No sense in all of them being awake at the ass crack of dawn.

He let himself into Packer's house, the front room more familiar than the one he'd lived in with Calleigh. How messed up was that?

He headed into the kitchen, smiling at the smell of fresh coffee, the note on the counter under a plate with a piece of cake wrapped up on it. He knew there'd be a sandwich in the fridge, too, and that the note said, 'Wake me up when you get home.'

He poured some coffee and unwrapped the cake. Life was short. Dessert first.

"Mmm." A soft, warm body pressed against him, hands sliding around his belly. "Ades. You're here."

Her breasts flattened against his back, her lips on his shoulder, and Adrian moaned a little. "Hey, baby girl. You feel good."

"Uh-huh." She snuggled, hands exploring him. "Missed you."

"I missed you, too." He had. He'd missed her like a sore tooth.

"Good." She worked his T-shirt out of his jeans.

"Yeah?" Hello. Someone was more than missing him. Someone was wanting.

"Uh-huh. This okay?" She was like fire behind him.

"Yeah, baby. More than." He loved how she could take

charge sometimes, how she took what she wanted. It sure had sparked their relationship again, her hunting him down.

"Oh, good. I need to feel you." She slid one hand up, fingers teasing his nipple, while the other cupped his cock.

"I need you too. Been so long since anyone touched me." He chuckled. "Well, Cotton helped me get the crayfish Landon put down my trousers."

Her laughter tickled his skin. "I want you to fuck me, Ades. The vibrator is fun, but I need a real cock." Filthy-mouthed girl.

"Well, come around here. I can't get to you back there." He tugged at her.

She slipped around, her hair all wild around her, sweet, curvy body dressed in one of Packer's shirts. *Oh, fuck yeah.*

He loved that look, spent a moment admiring. Then he took it off. He wanted her bare. She let him, then started unzipping his fly, bottom lip caught between her teeth. Lovely woman. She loved to undress him. She'd said it was like unwrapping a present.

He reached out, fingers smoothing her hair, tangling the littlest bit in the softness of it.

She glanced up at him from under her lashes, and Adrian smiled. "So pretty, baby."

She worked his jeans open, smoothing them and his briefs down past his ass. "Love you, Ades." She slid south, lips wrapping around his cock, just like that.

"Calleigh! Oh, God." His hands really tangled up in her hair, but Adrian didn't push. He let her do her thing, his hips rocking back and forth.

She moaned for him, around his dick. God, she knew how to get to him. Adrian spread his legs as much as he could, bracing on the kitchen counter. His hand barely missed smashing his cake. Fuck, her mouth. So hungry, taking him in, making his balls ache.

"Sweet. So hot, so good."

She brought him to the edge, then backed off, breathing

hard. "Need you, now. 'Kay?"

"Uh-huh. Get up here." He pulled her up, spinning them so her back was to the kitchen counter. He lifted her, stepping between her thighs.

She helped him out, hopping up and wrapping her legs around his hips. Thank God his girl was in shape.

He put her on the counter and rubbed against her, his cock finding her easily. She was wet for him, so hot. She nodded, leaned back a little so he could look down the front of her—hard nipples, flat belly with the ring, sweet bright red curls. She was a sight. Enough to make a man moan and twist. He pushed up, moving her so his dick prodded at her entrance.

She scooted closer, her wet folds slipping over him, driving him crazy. Adrian lifted her a tiny bit more, then pulled her down. Yes. He was inside her.

"Ades!" Her heels dug into his ass, her nails into his shoulder.

"That's it, baby girl. Let's ride." She had good leverage and they got going fast.

"Oh, fuck. Fuck, Ades. So fucking good." He loved how she loved to fuck, loved how she gave it up to him.

She bounced, and he shifted so he could hold her ass with one hand, his other sliding up around her belly to her breasts. Yeah. Soft and sweet.

"Mmm." She arched, one hand landing on the counter behind her.

"Uh-huh. Love your skin." He could eat her up.

"Love your cock, Ades. Please. Harder." Demanding girl.

He was happy to oblige, though. He moved faster, harder, really giving it to her. His hips tilted, his ass clenching as he thrust.

He could feel her orgasm around his cock, see the flush climbing up her belly.

"Fuck." Adrian moaned, the weeks alone on the road catching up with him all at once, his breath whooshing out as he came.

"Oh. Oh, fuck yeah." Calleigh's breath hitched, and she shook a little.

Adrian panted, his legs shaking. "Love that, baby girl."

"Mmm. Glad you're home." She slid off him, staying close.

"Me too." Adrian looped an arm around her, kicking the clothes off his one foot. He grabbed his cake with the other hand. "Couch?"

She scooped up a bite of frosting. "Bed."

"Yeah? I wouldn't want to wake Pack." But he went. He needed to see Packer, too.

"He's sleeping hard." She led him into the room, into the big bed.

Packer sure was sleeping hard, propped up so the collarbone and leg had support. There was still room for all of them.

Calleigh disappeared into the bathroom while he got settled careful in the spot that Calleigh'd left.

"Adrian?" Packer's eyes opened, the man blinking slow. "Hey, Chook."

"Hey, mate. You're a sight for sore eyes." He leaned up, took a slow kiss.

Packer hummed, kissed him back, one hand coming up behind his head.

"Mmm. Pack." Oh, he was a lucky bugger. First his baby girl, now his best mate.

"Taste like cake." Packer laughed. "Calleigh makes good tea and cake, huh?"

"She does."

Calleigh came out with a warm washrag to clean him up. "You want a piece, Pack? There's more."

"Don't go off just for me." Packer stroked Adrian's hair. "I'll have a bite of the Chook's."

Adrian nodded. "Come here, baby girl." He patted the bed. "We'll all share."

Calleigh smiled at them, sliding into the bed, easy as pie. Packer made this happy noise, and God, it was good to have them both.

"Mmm." Calleigh settled behind him, curled against his back, hand on his belly.

"Love you. Love being home." He snuggled, Packer's hand sliding over his shoulder.

"Chook. We missed you."

He felt Calleigh's nod against his back.

"Did you. Did you talk about me all night?" He grinned when they both pinched him.

"We pined." Calleigh's laugh made him happy.

"Oh, I like pining. That sounds fine."

Packer rolled his eyes, slipping his hand back to touch Calleigh for a second.

"What, mate? I need to know I'm loved." Adrian laughed because they were poking him in concert.

"Listen to you." Calleigh goosed him again. "Eat your cake so we can all get some sleep. I have to get up and help feed in the morning."

"Domestic woman. What do you know about feeding?" Calleigh was a city girl, he was pretty sure.

"I'm not stupid, Ades." She smacked his ass, hard. "Rob showed me what to do. He's off tomorrow and the next day."

"Mmm." He wiggled, to show her how much he appreciated that.

"Slut." Her hand reached down, cupped his balls and tugged.

His eyes rolled, his body reacting like he'd had a long dry spell, which he had. "Uh-huh."

Packer made a great noise, amused and horny. "Good thing you're cute."

"And I rode him hard, too." Calleigh's hand was wicked smart on him.

"Did you, love? Well, now, Chook. She can flat wear a man out."

"Has she been good to you, mate?" He wasn't jealous, more sad that he'd missed it.

"She has." Packer patted his hip. "We figured it."

"Mmmhmm." Her hand was still moving, rubbing him up and down, the touch sure and steady.

Adrian gritted his teeth, pushing into her hand, which rocked him against Packer. "Oh, God."

"Wanting man." Calleigh's nipples teased his back, Packer's strength his front.

"I know, I know." He wasn't ashamed of it, either.

Packer chuckled, good leg moving against him. Jesus, it was hot, being caught between them. He knew they couldn't do all the acrobatic things he had in mind, but it didn't matter. Packer and Calleigh were warm and there and ready to touch.

Besides that, he was bone-tired and Packer's mouth was like liquid sex, with Calleigh's hands slowly making him insane. Packer kissed him again and again, tongue pushing in, telling him all sorts of secrets. His Packer smelled like Calleigh's soap.

God. He was feeling warm and wanted, maybe a little pampered.

Calleigh kept stroking him, Packer kept his mouth busy, and Adrian let himself sink into it. He moaned, shifting, getting more skin, more touches. More kisses.

"Love you, Ades." Lips teased the curve of his ear.

"Baby." He bucked, needing more. His hands searched for skin.

He found Packer, the warm, fuzzy body solid under his palm. *Yeah. Yeah, feel that.* Hot and good, and Calleigh was soft and sweet behind him. He rocked back and forth.

"Gonna come again, Ades? Gonna shoot, then sleep with us?"

"Yeah. Yeah. I need to." He rubbed and pushed and his balls drew up and Adrian bit Packer, just a bit, on the upper arm.

Calleigh's free hand slid down his crease, fingertips teasing his hole.

Packer chuckled when he groaned. "She has such good

114

hands, Chook. Let it happen."

"You been...been having her touch?" Lucky fucker.

"Some, yeah. Come on, Chook." Packer took his mouth, making him want to scream.

Then the tip of Calleigh's finger pressed inside him, stroking him enough to make his fucking toes curl.

Adrian came so hard his teeth rattled, his cum spreading over Packer's skin.

"Mmm. Chook. Been missing that." Packer rubbed him right in, even as Calleigh drew the blankets up over them.

"I missed you. Both of you." He wanted to say more, but he was so sleepy. His eyelids were so heavy.

"Mmm. Love you, Ades. See you in the morning..." Calleigh cuddled in, sighing softly.

"Love you, baby girl. Night..." He dropped off, surrounded by the people he loved the most.

Finally.

* * * *

Packer woke up stiff and hot, but once he realized that Adrian was there, he relaxed. Not that he'd minded waking up with Calleigh. No, sir. They hadn't gotten past the point of not knowing how the other would wake up, yet. Adrian he could poke with impunity.

"Chook. I got to pee."

"Well, then, go. I ain't holding your pecker."

"I can't get up." He was in that bed chair thing, and he had come all over his belly...

Calleigh's laughter was soft, and he blinked over. She was up, dressed, shit, she'd probably worked for three hours already. "Come on, Pack. I'll help you. Ades, shift your ass."

"Thanks, luv." He really did love how Calleigh took charge of things sometimes. It was a quality he admired.

She grabbed him and got him moving, patting him on the ass. Packer chuckled, clumping to the loo, and he heard

Adrian grunt. Maybe she'd poked him, too.

He did his business, brushed his teeth and all, the scent of coffee making him smile.

"Here's a cup, Pack."

"Thanks, luv." He was fresher now and felt like he could give her a kiss. He did love a soft, warm set of curves against him. He kissed her nice and slow, his good hand going down to her butt. He needed some good morning. Her sweet arse pressed into his hand, rubbing in a little circle.

"Hello, luv." He grinned before he kissed her again.

"You two are starting without me!" Adrian came in, bumping Calleigh on the way.

"Oi. You wanted to sleep in." He wasn't going to let Adrian get off easy.

"You're both lazy." Calleigh's voice teased them both.

"Uh-huh. We're men." He was happy all of a sudden, even if he was still all gimpy.

"You don't say..." Calleigh's fingers teased his balls.

"I do." His voice might have gone up an octave.

Calleigh's husky laugh made him ache.

Adrian moved in closer, all three of them touching, swaying together. Adrian's hand slid over his ass, stroking in a lazy circle.

"Oh, now. You'll make me fall." His knees were weak from them already.

"No falling. I'm working on healing you up."

"I like how you work." He smiled for her, wanting her to know how good it was to have her there.

Look at that sheila go pink. That made him chuckle and lean for another kiss. He did love to kiss. Some blokes didn't, which Packer thought was right odd. Boy or girl, there was something to love about the slide of lips and tongues. Adrian pushed closer, stubble scraping him, tongue sliding into the kiss.

"Oh." The tiny noise escaped him, his hands moving as much as they could, his body swaying.

He had one hand around Calleigh's jeans-clad hip, the other on Adrian's bare skin. Fuck, that was fine. He let them hold him, and hold him up, because he wasn't sure he could do it alone. The tastes of them, the textures, were fucking perfect.

"You want the bed?" Calleigh moaned against his mouth.

"I do. Please." Oh, God, he wanted to be able to do everything, right now. Too bad his body wouldn't let him.

"Come on, Ades. Help me out." Calleigh started moving him, solid as a rock beside him.

They got him back to the bed, got him laid out and comfy, then set to driving him stark raving. They were like the best kind of tag team. Adrian was teasing his cock, their girl was at his nipple, biting and licking. Packer couldn't seem to make his arms move, and his leg was like lead, so he let them have at him. He'd pay them back when he could.

He felt Adrian's low moan as the tip of his cock was wrapped in heat. Fuck, yeah.

"Oh, fuck. Chook. Calleigh." His head spun with how good it all felt.

Calleigh headed north, her sweet, swollen lips offered to him for a kiss. Packer smiled against her mouth before he took control of the one thing he could. He was gonna eat her up.

Adrian took him down to the root even as Calleigh opened up to him, gave him her hot mouth. Packer moaned, kissing her, his hips pushing his dick up into Adrian's lips. It was like the best kind of torture. Adrian rolled his balls, pushing a little, giving him what he needed. Packer grunted, his injuries pulling as he arched and twisted, but God damn, how could he not? He was dying here.

Calleigh took his hand, brought it to her full, heavy breast. Packer squeezed, loving on her, his fingers finding her nipple. She moaned and Adrian swallowed, rubbing behind his balls.

"Oh, fuck. Please." Had he already begged? He gave Calleigh another squeeze, gave Adrian his cock, all the way down. Fuck, yes.

"Come on. Come for us."

Packer gritted his teeth to hold back the shout. Then he did what Calleigh had asked and shot like there was no tomorrow.

Calleigh chuckled softly, nuzzled into his throat.

"Melted." He tried to pat Adrian's head with his free hand. He couldn't move.

Calleigh chuckled and kissed him again, then moved to tackle Adrian. "What about you, Ades? Are you melted?"

Adrian reached down and grabbed a double handful of ass, like Packer wished he could. "No, love. I'm rarin' to go."

He did have one hell of a vantage point, though, with her straddling his Chook like that. Adrian's cock rubbed against her belly, and Packer was mesmerized, watching their skin together. Adrian leaned up and took one of her nipples in his mouth, cheeks hollowing as he sucked. Calleigh scooted closer, one hand cradling Adrian's head. Fuck, it was like watching the best kind of porn. Only he could smell them, could still taste them. And one of Adrian's hands was on his good leg, stroking his skin.

He jumped, his cock trying valiantly to rise again. "Sweet. Both of you."

Calleigh stared over at him, her eyes all dazed and shit. "Pack. Fuck, he's got a sweet mouth." Randy sheila.

"He does, luv. I bet it still tastes like me."

"Tastes like us, now." Her words obviously got Adrian to sucking harder, because Calleigh jerked, a flush climbing up her chest.

"God, Chook." He kept staring at the place where Adrian's mouth met Calleigh's skin. "Sweet girl."

Adrian looked at him, nodded, then switched nipples, the one he left behind hard and dark and shining. Packer reached up to touch it, barely reaching, pinching it between his fingers.

"Oh…" Those sounds drove him wild.

"Mmm." Adrian was making some amazing noises, too, grunting, pushing.

"Want... Fuck, boys..."

"Adrian. Chook. You heard her, huh? She wants you to fuck her." He grinned when they both moaned for him.

"Now. Now would be good."

"Yeah?" Adrian had pulled away from Calleigh's breast. "Okay, baby girl."

Calleigh leaned against his good side. "This okay?"

"This is better than okay."

She turned her head, nuzzled his skin. "Good."

"Sweet luv." She was a doll. Adrian was more of a devil.

Adrian chuckled, bent and nipped at her. Packer felt every move she made, every quiver of her muscles. She was so soft, so different from them.

Adrian moved between her thighs, his cock hard and proud, eyes dragging over the both of them. "Shit."

"Come on, Chook. Give her what for." He grinned, giving Adrian a dare with his eyes.

He got a wild grin, then Adrian took himself in hand, rubbing against her clit.

Calleigh moaned, wiggled. "Ades..."

"That's it. Come on, luv. Ride him good."

"Yes. Ades. Fuck me. Want your cock."

He loved the way Adrian's eyes crossed when she talked dirty to him. Made his own eyes cross a little, too. Packer loved a dirty girl.

Adrian grabbed one of her legs, spread her, then pushed in, filling her in one quick thrust. The sound of it was amazing, like the smell of them together.

"Ades. Again." He could see her nails digging into Adrian's shoulder.

"Yeah. Baby girl."

Packer loved how Adrian called her that. Adrian fucked her like he meant it, like he knew she wouldn't break. It was the hottest thing ever. God, if he ever got to see her spank Adrian's ass again he might die.

She gasped, tossed her head, and that long red hair covered his cock.

"Oh, God." Yeah. Death was imminent.

He got his free hand moving, sliding that hair on his skin. Soft, silky, it was perfect on him, around him.

"Boys. Y'all…" Look at her move. She was talking for them, moaning.

"Sweet luv." He was so damned ready to get his body back.

"So fucking hot, baby." Adrian was a fucking machine, driving into her.

Packer was moving with them, Calleigh's hair like an amazing caress.

"Need y'all. I. Damn." Calleigh arched, driving herself down faster.

"Come on, baby girl." Adrian drove into her, hands on her skin, dark against her pale.

She nodded, hair dancing on his skin again and again. "Close."

"Yeah. Yeah, baby." Adrian did something with his hand that made Calleigh cry out, her body shaking. *God, look at her come.*

Packer groaned, reached out, tugged one nipple. She was so warm, so good against his hand. Adrian's hips moved hard and fast, eyes rolling back into his head as he shook.

"Chook. Look at you." He managed one smack to Adrian's butt before the man finished up, drawing a moan.

"Damn. Damn." Adrian panted, smiled at him.

He was a lucky, lucky man. And he knew it.

* * * *

"Calleigh! Baby girl? Where the fuck are you?"

Calleigh frowned from the barn where she was feeding cattle. Rob had shown her what to do, how to do it. It wasn't too hard, easier than she remembered.

"In the barn, Ades. What do you want?"

"What are you doing in the barn?" He came in, blinking at the change in the light.

"Working. What's up?" She hefted the feed bag, poured the sweet feed into the bucket.

Ades stared at her. "You're a nurse."

"I know. Did you hit your head at the last event?"

"No, baby. I didn't think you knew anything about horses."

"I grew up on a ranch, dork, and Rob showed me how." She chuckled, feed sprinkling everywhere.

"Oh." His face drew up in a frown. "How did I not know that?"

Calleigh shrugged. "It never came up. Mom and Dad are gone. It's a thing." She'd walked away and gone to work.

"It never came up." He blinked again. "That's like me saying it never came up that my dad was a helicopter pilot."

"Ades, it's not like we talked a lot." She put the feed bag down, stumbling under the weight of it.

"Shit, baby." Ades righted her. "Why don't you tell me what to do out here and go help Packer do his thing? That was why I came looking. He's like a bear with a sore paw."

"Thank you." She lifted her face for a kiss. "What's wrong with him? Just bored?"

"He hates needing help. And for some reason it makes him rage-y when I'm the one helping." Adrian smiled a little. "He's a guy."

"Yep." She poked his belly, hard. "Kiss me."

Adrian grinned all of a sudden, the expression happy and horny. Then he grabbed her by the waist and pulled her close, laying a good one on her.

Oh, yummy. She opened up, tongue sliding against his. Humming, he tugged her closer, lifting her against his chest and hips. He was so warm. Ades kissed her like he meant it, like he wanted her melted and crazy and right there. It was amazing, to feel that again, to know he still needed her.

"God damn it, where are you two buggers?" Packer's voice rang out and she giggled, dove back into Adrian's kiss.

Adrian laughed against her lips, squeezing her butt. "He's whipping up a foam."

"He's more bark than bite. You're bitchy, Pack. What's up?" She made sure he could hear her.

"Where the hell is my blue shirt?" He was bellowing like a bull moose.

She snorted. "Like he's only got one. Boys."

Adrian swatted her butt. "Hey!"

Calleigh cracked up, then kissed his nose. "I better go help before he gets his feelings hurt."

"Yeah. I'll finish up in here, huh?"

"Thanks. Love you." She kissed the side of his mouth, headed out to the thundering cloud. "What're you so pissy about, Pack?"

Packer was teetering on his good leg, his pajamas all askew. "Where did everyone go?"

"I was feeding for you." She scooted under his arm, gave him something to lean on. "Mmm. You smell good."

"I feel like a useless piece of shit, luv." He clumped along, letting her lead him back to the house.

"You need a hobby, honey. Something to do with your hands." She grabbed his shirt on their way through the laundry room.

"How?" He waved his good arm. "The damned collarbone…"

"Are you a reader? I have a Kindle and you can turn pages one-handed."

"I like to read." That actually seemed to perk up his interest. "Yeah."

"Cool. Let me delete some books and I'll give it to you." No way was she admitting to reading some of the stuff she had.

"Delete?" He raised a brow, grinning at her now.

She hoped she wasn't blushing too much. "Uh-huh. To, uh, free you some room up."

"Oh, I'll read anything." He was a shithead. He really

was. Pack had to know she was hiding something.

"Let me… I'll grab it." Her fucking face was burning.

"No worries, luv." He kissed her cheek, relenting a bit.

She turned her face and brought their lips together for a second, then went to find her Kindle, delete the more perverse titles. A girl had to keep her secrets, after all.

Packer had managed to get into a pair of sweats by the time she got back, but the shirt was half on, his bad side defeating him. Poor baby.

"Here, let me help." She got him dressed and settled into his chair quick as a flash.

"Thanks, luv." He sighed. "Ready to be better."

"I bet you are." She got her fingers on his neck and started working his muscles, leaning over the soft back of the chair.

"Yeah." He grunted, his head dipping so she could work good. "Thanks."

"Mmmhmm. So tense. You need to relax." She hoped it wasn't her, stressing him out.

"I hate this." He chuckled, reaching with his good hand to pat her wrist. "You should go on and spend some time with Adrian. I have the books, the remote, huh?"

"As soon as the critters are fed, I'm going to sit on my butt and paint my toenails."

He hummed. "Can I watch?"

She chuckled. He liked to watch her do all sorts of things. "You can." Perv.

"Brilliant. Go on, do my work."

"Spoiled brat." She kissed the edge of his ear.

"Uh-huh. You wait until I got both arms and both legs."

"Then you'll have to chase me."

"Oh, luv. Then I'll take you down like a footballer."

She snorted. "A tight end?"

"A what?"

Oh, right. He thought of football as something completely different. "Foreigner." She goosed him. "I can't believe they let you live in Texas."

"I'm a cowboy. Of course they do." He winked back at

her, wincing when something pulled.

"Ow. Easy, Pack. Rest. Let me make some coffee."

"Okay." He sighed, leaning back in his chair, and she got the feeling maybe he'd worn himself out a bit when Adrian got home.

She headed to the kitchen, whistling under her breath, waving at Adrian in the yard. Adrian waved back, flashing her a wide, white grin before getting back to hauling some feed.

It was a little weird, but she was happy.

Really, truly happy.

* * * *

Adrian stretched, enjoying the burn along the backs of his shoulders. It felt good to work, to get some time in at the ranch. Help Pack out. It felt good to be with Calleigh, too. Shit, he'd never seen her ride a horse before. It was inspiring.

Pack was sitting out on the back porch, beer in hand, mouth hanging open as they stared at Calleigh. "Look at her, Chook."

"I know!" Adrian shook his head. "I had no idea."

"It's damn hot, really."

She was flying, exercising one of the roans, both of them going flat out. "It is," Adrian agreed. There was so much he didn't know about his girl.

"Wonder what she'd do on a little bull—"

"Stop it." No way. His girl was a girl, through and through.

"What? She's a strong sheila."

"She's not a guy," Adrian said. Packer was so weird sometimes.

"No. No, I seen all her bits…"

"Then no riding bulls."

Packer snorted. "Sexist."

"Fucker. Am not. She's not meant to do that shit."

"Why not? She can tote feed," Packer pointed out.

"Yeah, well, I'm here now. I'll do it." He chuckled, grinned at Pack. "You should have seen her in the barn lugging that bag around."

"I should have." Pack grunted, face clouding over. "Fucking useless, I am."

He stared at Packer. "Don't be a wanker. Next time, stay out from under the bull."

Packer blinked, then broke into that amazing grin that transformed his whole face. "Yeah, yeah."

They watched Calleigh go, and Adrian saw it before it happened, the little roan headed for the fence, full-bore, intending to jump it, or try to.

"Shit." Packer was struggling to get up, but neither of them was gonna help. Calleigh pulled the mare up, but went right over the horse's ears, flopping on the ground.

"God damn it! Calleigh!" Adrian took off at a dead run, while Calleigh slowly sat up. He skidded to a stop next to her, batting the anxious roan away so those hooves didn't hurt anyone. "Baby?"

"I'm okay." She was a little teary and there were going to be bruises, but she reached for him easily.

"You hit hard, baby girl. You're a cowboy." That ought to make her smile.

"I'm good." She stood up, brushed her backside off with shaky hands.

"You are. I didn't know you could ride like that, huh?" He grabbed the reins, pulling the roan up short.

"Yeah, but did you know I could fall off so well?" She reached for the mare, murmuring softly, calming her.

"You did great. Packer thinks you should ride bulls, yeah, mate?"

Packer was slowly making his way across the yard. "No fucking way! You hurt, girl? Come here, let me see!"

Adrian hid a grin. Fussy old bastard.

Calleigh's cheeks pinked. "I'm fine."

"I said come here, damn it."

Calleigh headed to the fence.

"You want him to fall and break something else, baby?" Adrian asked. Packer was more stubborn.

"No!" She went to Pack and Pack tugged her in, tilted her face up to stare at it.

"You okay, luv?" Packer studied his girl, really looking her over.

"Just a little rattled." Bruises were going to be blooming on her face in a few hours, but right now she had a smile for Pack.

"Let Adrian walk the mare out, luv. Come get some ice on that."

"I..."

Pack grumbled. "Now, Calleigh. Chook, you good?"

"I am." Adrian would turn the horse over to the wrangler, who should be doing the exercising in the first place, and make sure his girl was okay.

Packer herded Calleigh back toward the house, rumbling softly all the way. It was bloody adorable, how Pack could turn the tables and take care of someone.

Adrian handed off the mare, headed toward the house.

Calleigh sat in Packer's chair, a cold beer pressed to her cheek. "I'm okay," she said.

"Where's Pack?"

"Getting her an ice pack." Packer hobbled out of the back door, holding an ice pack.

"I told him I'd be fine."

"Let me cluck for a change," Pack said. "I get to turn the tables."

Adrian chuckled. "Yeah. It's fun to watch."

His ass was popped, hard. Adrian jumped, the sting making his breath catch. He'd never hear the end of it if anyone but Pack and his girl found out how he felt about that.

Pack went to Calleigh, took his beer and handed over the ice pack. "Damn it, your sweet face."

"She'll be all right, mate." Adrian nudged Pack down into

the porch swing.

"The mare just got away from me is all. It's been a while."

"You looked good, luv." Pack wasn't much on compliments like that. He really liked Calleigh.

"Thanks." She smiled over, eyes dancing a little bit. "I'll get better."

Adrian cackled. "She needs practice."

"No more practice falling." Pack sounded sure.

"No, just riding," Adrian agreed. "You. Me."

Packer groaned. "I could get behind that, Chook, that sweet girl around my cock."

Calleigh stared at him, her thighs rubbing together. Adrian grinned, feeling a pleasant tightness in his groin. Nice.

"You okay, Ades?"

"Huh? Yeah. Just horny."

"Didn't you get enough already?" Calleigh asked.

Silly chick. Like there was ever enough. "What?" He winked at Packer. Packer grinned back.

She chuckled, shook her head. "Horndogs."

"We're boys, huh?" Adrian figured it was a byproduct of maleness.

"Yes." Those pretty green eyes looked them both up and down. Approving. Damn. She was something else, his girl. So hot.

Packer groaned, shifted. "That's not fair, to stare at a bloke that way."

"It's only not fair if she's not gonna follow through." Adrian knew better with his girl. His Calleigh wasn't a cock tease, not even at her meanest.

"She's all beat up." Packer still seemed pretty worried on that.

"She's nowhere near as busted as you." Or as him, for fuck's sake.

Packer stared at him.

"She's sitting right here!" Calleigh said, snorting.

Adrian chuckled. "And she's grumpy."

127

"Well, I can't blame her. She needs a cuppa and a nice hot shower."

"Mmm. I might take a shower. Packer, you should have a hot tub here."

"Oh, that's a good idea."

Adrian blinked from Packer to Calleigh. One suggestion from her and it's a good idea? What the fuck?

"What?" Packer stared at him, the corner of that pretty mouth curling up.

"You..." Fucker. Packer was a fucker. Adrian had been after him to put in a hot tub for years.

"Me. Hot tub. I like it."

"Me too. We could bubble." Calleigh seemed like butter wouldn't melt in her mouth.

"We so could. We could all fit, too." Packer gave him a raised brow. "See, we never needed it before because we'd both fit in the bath."

"Mmm. I like it. All of us. Lights. Beer." Calleigh hummed, nodded.

"We just needed a reason." Packer chuckled. "I can write it off as rehab."

Calleigh's laugher was sweet as sugar. "There you go!"

"I like it." Adrian nodded. Tomorrow they could go hunting for a hot tub for three.

Calleigh stood, winced a little, her bruises starting to show. "Gonna grab a shower, y'all."

"Want me to come with?" He gave Pack an apologetic glance, but he wasn't above taking advantage.

"You going to wash my back for me, Ades?"

"Hell, yeah." He waited for Packer to wave him on, a wry grin on that expressive face. Then he took Calleigh's arm.

"So did I look like a total idiot out there?"

"What? No. You looked amazing, baby girl." Adrian helped her strip off, wincing at some of the bruises he'd not seen yet.

"It felt good. Fun."

"Good on you. I had no idea." He got her boots off when

they hung her jeans up. God, she was something — so little for as strong as she was. When she was bare he got the water going and stripped off his own kit, reaching for her as soon as he could. "You need that hot shower, baby."

"I do." She moved into his hands immediately, let him hold her.

Adrian hummed, getting her in the shower. Pack had a nice big one with two shower heads. It rocked.

The water hit her and she moaned, pretty skin going silky for him.

"Look at you. Missed you, baby girl." Adrian bent to lick a few drops off her shoulder.

"Missed you, too. We both did." Her nipples tightened, just like that.

"Yeah? Good." He was selfish enough to want both of them to need him. He wanted to have his cake and eat it, too.

"Mmmhmm." She leaned in, rubbing along him, slick and warm.

Her breasts felt soft against his chest, her nipples hard little points. He'd always loved that, the way she responded to him.

"Open the curtain, Chook. Want to watch." Packer's voice was low, husky.

Adrian's scalp prickled, his cock pressing harder against Calleigh's belly. "We'll get water all over."

"The floor'll mop. Open the fucking curtain," Pack demanded.

Calleigh snuggled in, giggling softly.

Adrian laughed, pondering teasing Pack a bit more. That was mean, though, as the man was less than mobile. "All right, mate. Here." He opened the curtain halfway.

"Oh, you two are a sight. Turn a bit, now. Let me see her backside."

Adrian grunted, his feet slipping, clumsy with his need. He got them turned, though, so Pack could see. Calleigh wasn't helping, those hands sliding down his back, nails teasing a little. Adrian tried to go up on tiptoe, bracing against the wall with the hand not holding Calleigh's butt.

"Horny thing," Calleigh murmured. One of her hands cupped his balls.

"He's always horny, yeah, luv?" Packer had moved to lean against the sink, good hand pressing against his crotch.

"Always." Calleigh turned her face up for his kiss.

Adrian took it, only thinking for a moment about the show they were putting on. Then he got lost in the taste of her. Fuck, her mouth was like heaven, tongue sliding along his, kissing him right back. He did love the way his girl kissed him. She wasn't afraid to eat him up.

"Spread her a little now." Packer was a demanding bastard. Still, it was a good plan. Adrian lifted one of Calleigh's legs. "Look at that. Wet and pink."

Calleigh shivered, stepped closer.

"Mmm. She feels good, Pack. Hot."

"Y'all…" Mmm. He liked that sound in his girl's voice.

"So pretty. She's so pretty, Adrian. Touch her for me."

His fingers slid down her ass, spread her a little wider. Packer moaned, shifting around. Bless his heart, it had to be hard to get comfortable.

"Everything okay, Pack?" Calleigh leaned back, grinned at Packer upside down.

"Uh-huh." Damned if Pack didn't ease forward and kiss her mouth, short and sweet but pretty. The position did amazing things to her boobs.

Adrian ducked his head, rubbed his stubbly chin across one nipple.

Calleigh moaned for him, her hands on his shoulders, nails digging in. Tingles slid right down his spine.

"Don't you drop her, now, Chook."

"No. No, I got her." He did. His footing was solid now and he had Calleigh in a good grip. He could feel Pack's hand sliding between her legs, touching her, teasing her folds. Adrian panted, pressing harder against her soft skin, needing friction all of a sudden. His cock slid along the crack of her ass and he grabbed her hips, keeping her close.

"Love that. Love how you feel, baby girl." Adrian kissed her skin, licked up water.

"Uh. Uh-huh…" She shuddered, then propped one leg on the side of the tub.

"Fuck." The awe in Pack's voice was something else. Shivery good.

"Please, y'all. Keep touching."

"We won't let you down, baby." He held her up with one arm, his other moving so his fingers could find Pack's.

"No. No, you won't. Oh, fuck."

His fingers found Packer's, the man's callused fingertips drawing little circles around her swollen clit. Adrian grinned, knowing that had to be driving his girl crazy. She was wet as could be, and not from the shower. He flicked gently over the tip of that sweet little bundle of nerves, barely teasing, and Calleigh jerked like he'd touched her with a live wire.

"She's ready to go off like a rocket, Chook."

He slowed down, eased off, loving the needy whimper that got him. Packer chuckled, and he could feel those fingers move, pushing down.

"Y'all are so fucking mean." Calleigh sounded desperate.

"No, luv." Pack hummed. "We're making it last."

"And last and last." He nudged her clit again, carefully, knowing it wasn't enough.

"Ades!" She all but climbed his body, with Packer offering just enough support to steady them.

Adrian grinned. "Yeah, baby girl?"

"I'll beat your ass. Make me come, y'all."

"Mmm. Want to see that." Packer slipped his fingers inside Calleigh's body.

"Mmm… Me come or me beat his ass?" Calleigh's hips started to rock.

"Both, luv."

He would swear he could feel Pack's breath on their skin.

"Oh. Oh." Her hips started moved, and he started working

her clit.

"Calleigh..." Adrian loved the way she rocked and panted, these sounds coming out of her.

"Please. Please. More." Wanton woman.

"We got more, luv. Right, Adrian?"

"Right." He slid one leg farther between hers, opening her, letting Packer really push those fingers in. Wet, slick, and blazing hot—God, he could sink himself balls deep inside her. She wasn't waiting for them, though.

She was roaring toward the finish line, humping them both, her breasts bouncing with the motion. She was fucking unbelievable. He leaned forward, mouth on her shoulder, biting down. The whole time his eyes were on Packer.

Packer grinned for him, cheeks hot, eyes sparkling. The man might not have both hands but he was making her writhe. Beautiful motherfucking man.

Calleigh cried out, jerked against him, her sweet ass rubbing his dick. He massaged her clit a little harder, wanting her to come for them, needing her so bad. He felt her, heard her as she came, dissolving for them.

"Fuck." Packer breathed the word, smiling at them both, hot as fire.

He nodded, holding her up as she shivered. Packer sat back, good hand sliding away from Calleigh's body to rub that hard dick.

"If you lie on the bed, Pack, I'll ride you," Calleigh told Packer.

"Okay." There was no argument there, and Pack damned near killed himself getting up.

She turned in Adrian's arms, kissed him. "You too. Come to bed."

"Mmmhmm." God, yes. Like he would miss that.

Calleigh grabbed a towel and helped Pack while he turned the water off, grabbed a towel for himself. Somehow they all made it to the bed together, him and Calleigh helping Pack get settled. It would have been sweet but for Pack's amazing hard-on.

"Gonna let me ride you?"

Calleigh moved to straddle Packer and Adrian moved behind her, to support her, hold her up so they didn't hurt that broken collarbone.

Packer moaned, body moving under them, trying to find sensation.

He could smell Calleigh, and that sweet, heady scent got stronger as his girl reached down and slipped the tip of Packer's cock through her folds.

"Oh." Packer made this amazing noise, and Adrian had to smile. That and touch both of them.

"Mmmhmm." She shifted, scooted forward, then eased herself down and Packer's eyes rolled furiously.

"Lord, luv. Adrian, get up here." Pack's good hand reached past Calleigh's hip.

"I'm right here." He scooted closer, making sure to stabilize Calleigh's body.

"That's it. Right there." He could feel Packer now, when his dick slid down under Calleigh's ass.

"Oh." Calleigh stilled, shivered. "Y'all. Y'all…"

"Sweet luv." Pack was moving pretty hard, as banged up as he was, really giving it to her.

"Packer… Feels so good. Ades…" Calleigh shook her head back and forth, eyes rolling.

"Mmm. Good." Adrian rocked against her, against Pack, feeling skin on skin. Bloody amazing.

"Gonna both take her one day, Chook. You and me together, loving on our sweet girl."

Adrian could feel what Packer's words did to Calleigh, as she shivered and shook.

"Yeah." He leaned against her back, hand slipping down her belly, down to her clit. "Yeah. Both of us."

Calleigh was soaking wet, blazing hot, clit swollen and begging for more attention. Adrian rubbed it in tiny circles, listening to her moan. A dull flush climbed her belly, her nipples hard as nails as she bounced and rode. Packer was moaning, cussing, touching his hip, Calleigh's ribs. Adrian

133

could smell them, smell both of them, and moved his finger faster.

"Ades. Oh, fuck." Both of them were calling his name. It made him fly.

Calleigh started shifting, hands on the headboard now, driving herself back on Packer's dick.

It was like watching really good porn, only being able to participate. Man, if he could bottle this, he could make a million. But then he'd have to share and the thought made him growl. Not logical, but true.

Sharing with Calleigh and Pack made sense. They were his.

Calleigh reached back, one hand wrapping around his cock, pulling hard.

"Fuck. Fuck yes." Adrian rocked, hoping he wasn't hurting Pack with the vibrations.

They were all together now, in sync, moving hard.

Packer panted, Calleigh gasped, and Adrian thought it sounded like music. Maybe that was what people meant about making music together.

"Soon. Soon, y'all. Boys." Calleigh arched, rocked down hard.

"Yeah, baby girl. Come on, now." He knew Packer was ready to go, and Adrian could just wallow in them. He nipped the curve of Calleigh's shoulder and that was all it took, she hollered for them. She felt so sweet against him, shaking, her hips pushing her against his hand, against Packer's cock.

Packer growled deep in his throat, hips punching up, eyes rolling as he came.

"That's it, mate. Oh, fuck." Adrian came too, his cock rubbing that amazing ass of Calleigh's.

Calleigh's arms trembled, barely holding her up.

"I got you, baby." He held her, helping her off to one side so no one fell on Pack.

Pack grinned at him, damn near melted. "Shit, that's fine."

"Yeah. Yeah. Wait until you're better. It will be killer."

Calleigh chuckled, the bruises really starting to pop up on her fine skin.

Adrian stroked her skin, his hand moving slowly. "You all right, baby?"

"I'm good."

"She's going to be sore later, Chook. You got them muscle pills?"

"I do." Adrian rolled out of bed, going to get some hot towels, some muscle relaxers, and a drink for all of them. Something fizzy. He could hear Packer talking, soft and low, then he got back, and Calleigh was curled against his side, almost asleep.

"Poor baby." Adrian bent and kissed Calleigh's neck. "Here, Calleigh. Take these and you can sleep."

"Mmm, 'm okay, Ades. Don' need 'em."

Right.

Packer rumbled, popped her butt. "Now, girl."

"Ow! Supposed to be helping, not hurting…" But she did open up like a baby bird, didn't she?

He popped the pill in, gave her a sip of water.

"That's it, luv." Packer was smitten with his girl already. He knew that tone in his cowboy's voice.

Calleigh snuggled in, cuddling with Packer, eyelids heavy. Adrian turned off lights and made sure everything was good before crawling into bed. Calleigh felt soft and good, and Packer made a happy noise.

His eyes met Packer's and they both smiled.

Better.

Much, much better.

Chapter Ten

Calleigh wandered from store to store, whistling as she moved through the crowds on the Riverwalk. God, she loved San Antonio. They had a two-day invitational down here that Ades was riding in and Pack was getting the last of the casts off. Four weeks of rehab and he'd be back on the circuit, too.

Oh, look at those shoes...

She headed in, eyes on the prettiest pair of six-inch, leopard, peep toe pumps ever. She'd just gotten the left shoe on when her cell phone rang, Ades' number coming up.

"'Lo?" God, the shoes made her legs look great.

"Hey, baby girl! We have a free Packer. Where are you? We'll do lunch."

"Woo! I'm buying hooker shoes on the Riverwalk. Where are you?"

"Just back at the hotel. We could meet you. We'll take the boat taxi thing for Pack."

"Are you sure? There's a neat old Mexican restaurant right here." She let her voice drop. "I'll wear the shoes so you can see." She had a flirty mini skirt on, one of Packer's button-downs tied around her waist.

She heard a muffled conversation, then Packer laughed, loud and sexy. Adrian chuckled. "We'll be there. What's the restaurant?"

"Casa Rio. I'll be there in ten." She tried on another couple of pairs, then settled on the leopard ones. Perfect. She could feel her ass swaying from side to side as she moved.

"Calleigh Roberts. What are you doing here?"

She glanced back, met the eyes of Brandy Collins. "Buying shoes. You?"

"I'm here with the tour, of course." The girl dragged her gaze her up and down, lips pursing.

She resisted the urge to flip the little bitch off. "Make sure you cheer for my husband."

"Oh, I will." That sneer happened again.

"Look, do you have a problem with me? If you do, maybe you ought to just come out with it so we can put it to bed for once and for all." She didn't have the energy for this shit.

"A problem with you?" Brandy's lined-eyes went comically wide. "Why ever would I have a problem with a woman that's cheating on her husband with his best friend? I mean, that's not filthy, right?"

Calleigh forced herself not to rock back on her heels in utter shock. For chrissake. Seriously? No way was she letting this evil shit get the best of her. No fucking way.

She pushed up her sunglasses with her middle finger, making sure the gesture was explicitly clear and completely unmistakable.

Brandy gasped, hand flying to her lips in pure shock. Calleigh held her gaze, stared the girl down until she turned on her heel with a snarled, "I'll make you pay, bitch."

"See ya." That was way classier than 'Fuck off, you piece of shit whore'. Way classier. She tried hard to put the little snot out of her mind. It got way easier when she caught sight of a castless Packer heading her way.

She wolf whistled. "Look at you!"

Packer grinned, those fine lines crinkling up his face. "Look at those shoes, huh?"

She spun slowly, showing off. "Not bad, hmm?"

"Not bad doesn't cover it, baby girl." Adrian came right up and kissed her, smiling, hand on her hip.

"Mmm." One foot came up, just like in the movies.

Packer laughed, his mouth close to her ear, his hand on her butt. "Hungry?"

"Starving. You?" She met those dark, dancing eyes. "Tell

me you got the all clear from the doctor."

"I did."

Ades grinned. "He's supposed to avoid heavy lifting and hardcore cardio."

"Oh, man. No doing me then..." She winked.

"Fuck that." Packer growled a little, squeezing.

"Mmm. Feed me, cowboys." Yummy. They were both more tasty than any food. They walked into the Mexican place, a middle-aged waiter seating them and serving them chips. It was amazing how much better Pack seemed.

She sat beside Adrian, one peep toe sliding up Packer's leg. "So, no hardcore stuff, Pack? Shame..."

"Oh, gimme maybe two weeks of physio and I'll be right as rain." He winked.

She chuckled. "I'll have to play with Ades and keep him busy."

"Oh, now. No one said I couldn't do something."

Adrian's ears went red, and he ignored Packer. "What are you going to do, baby girl?"

She leaned in, tongue on his ear. "I could ride you. I could molest your sweet bod. I could make you lick me till I scream..." She refused to blush, damn it. Refused to. This was the new, bolder Calleigh.

Packer chuckled. "You could tie him up."

"I could. I could warm his pretty ass."

"Y'all!" Adrian tried to protest, but he sounded more intrigued than scandalized.

"Yes, Ades?" She leaned back, winked.

"Right here. Maybe I'll decide what I want, huh?"

"Oh, Pack and I pretty much know what you want."

Packer grinned, and it was pure evil. "Better yet, we know what you need, Chook."

God, it was good to have Pack better. He'd been so down, a little sullen and a lot like he felt useless. Now? That smile promised all sorts of things for both her and Adrian.

The waiter came back with chips and two beers and a margarita and they ordered — fajitas for the boys, a chicken taco plate for her.

"So, what's your draw tonight, Chook?" Packer munched a chip, so much happier.

"Bender. He's a good'un."

She had to reach over, squeeze Adrian's thigh. Ades jumped, then gave her a smile so warm it almost melted her. He'd gotten used to not having anyone around, she'd bet.

"I'll be in the stands, avoiding Brandy Collins and cheering loud."

Packer was the one to give her a glare. "She bothering you?"

"She wants Adrian. She hates me. It's nothing."

Ades flushed, shaking his head. "I have never encouraged her, baby."

"Ades." She met his eyes. "You're the prettiest son of a bitch on tour, and that includes the Brazilians. You don't have to encourage."

Packer grinned. "She's got a point there, Chook. You're irresistible."

She nodded. "Then there's Mister Sex on a Stick Please God Fuck Me Now across the table. Also, no encouragement required."

"I've only got two hands, love, and they're both full." Packer reached out to run one finger over the back of her hand. "Promise."

"Mmm." She grinned at both of them, as happy as she'd ever been.

They both seemed pretty darned happy, too. It made her warm, deep in her belly.

She leaned against Adrian a little. "Did y'all want me to make reservations for after the event or should we wing it?"

"We should probably go ahead and wing it, love. Might not be much open."

"Works for me. I'm flexible."

"You are." Adrian nudged her leg with his. "You always

139

could get in the best positions."

"Mmm. We should explore that, the three of us."

"I think so, yeah." The food came before anyone could get more down and dirty with the conversation, though, and Pack managed to look a touch disappointed.

They dug in, her offering bites, laughing together. It was nice, to be out and about with them, spending time. No weirdness, no pressure. They listened to her shopping experience from the morning, both pouting when they found out she'd resisted buying the sparkly hoochie mama dress.

"The shoes are a hit, though, luv." Packer fed her a spicy bite of shrimp. "If you don't wear them to the event, you'll have to put them back on in the room."

"Oh, I'll bring them in my bag for supper after. The stairs are a little intense in them."

"I like that idea." Ades leaned again, his arm brushing her breast. Evil man.

"You win money tonight, cowboy, and I'll wear whatever you want to supper."

"Yeah?" Adrian swallowed hard. "Better watch that, baby."

"You have my word, Ades." She winked.

Adrian moaned a little.

Packer snorted. "He's so easy."

"He is. I love that about him."

"We might have mentioned that before, huh?" Packer winked, licking his lower lip.

"Couple of times." She let one hand trail on Adrian's thigh.

Adrian jumped again for her, cheeks so hot, eyes like blue lasers. He was ready, and she hated to tell him no, but he still had to go ride.

"Tell me what you'll pick for me to wear, Ades."

"I like you in that lacy thing. The one that has the bra and the attached dress."

She pinked, smiled. "You got it." God, that one was

about a half yard of fabric, altogether. He got points for consistency, though. He'd always loved that one. "You want me to wear the diamond belly button ring, too?"

"Oh, God."

Packer rested his chin on his hand. "I think that's a yes."

"Yeah?" Damn, they made her feel like the hottest woman ever.

"Mmm. I know it is for me and I've never seen it."

"You should see her dance with it in, mate..." Adrian moaned.

Packer leaned close. "We should skip watching him ride and go to the hotel." Evil man. Look at that twinkle in Pack's eye.

She chuckled. Like Pack would walk away from a chance to be with the guys. The boys were bull-riders first, fuck-buddies second. She knew that.

It still made Adrian protest. "I don't think so, mate."

Packer snorted, hands patting his pockets for his smokes.

Adrian grinned at her. "Have you yelled at him yet?"

She blinked over, fluttered her eyelashes. "Would I do that?" She'd refused to go buy his cigarettes when he'd been laid up.

He'd been too doped up on pain pills to do much bitching, and while he'd puffed a few since then, he'd mostly broken the habit.

Adrian laughed and she reached out with her foot again, loving on Pack under the table. It was so good to have the cast off.

Packer shook his head mournfully. "Tobacco gets no respect. Do we get dessert?"

"You two do. I'm going to get fat, if I don't watch it."

"Not a chance." Ades kissed her cheek, and she was suddenly surrounded by warm male, the boys pressing in on either side.

"Oh..." She snuggled in. "Hey."

"Hey." Packer grinned at the beaming waiter who wandered over. "*Sopapillas, amigo.*"

"*Si, señor*. Six or nine?"

"Nine. Man needs his carbs today."

Adrian nodded. "Lots of honey."

"Sticky. I like it." Packer could do this growly thing that made her nipples go hard and she shifted, sliding on the seat.

Adrian laughed, the sound delighted. "Mmm. Look at you."

"All surrounded by cowboys with nowhere to go." She was a lucky girl.

"Nowhere to hide."

* * * *

Packer flexed his hands, pain not shooting down them for the first time in ages. His leg was a bit weak, still wrapped, but the cast was gone. And he was on the back of the chutes where he belonged, ready to help Adrian get ready to ride.

His Chook was loose-limbed, easy, still melted from the orgasm and the massage he'd gotten in the hotel room. Calleigh was a good luck charm for them. He was glad as hell they'd settled all the weirdness he'd caused, running her off with his big mouth.

"Pack! Man! How's the leg?" Little Cotton came be-bebopping by, the smile on his face almost obscene.

"Good. Not riding yet, y'know, but better." He clapped Cotton on the shoulder. "You look tickled."

"Am. My girl, she said yes, huh?"

"Yeah? Good on you!" He gave Cotton a one-armed hug. "You'll have to let me and Ades buy you a drink next time." This time they had plans after the show.

"Sure. Not today, though. Both of our families are in town. There's, like, a deal with brothers and Momma meeting."

"Well, there you go." He winked. He wondered if Calleigh had any family. Adrian had never said.

"Yeah. Adrian, man, you need someone to pull rope?" Cotton was a good 'un, through and through.

"I do. Pack can't get up on the fence yet, huh?" Adrian smiled at Cotton, and Pack blinked. Adrian was about as silly happy as Cotton.

"Nope. But he's standing. We'll take it." Cotton crawled over, whistling, and Adrian gave him a grin.

"Happy bastard."

"A soon to be married bastard." Pack grinned. Cotton's girl was…something.

"Yeah? Good on you, mate." Adrian climbed up and the jabber stopped. Leastways the serious stuff. This all was just noise. Packer stood next to the chute, his hand ready to catch Adrian should the bull lunge. He knew his arms were still not all that, so Kynan was there, too.

Bender was stomping some, giving the folks a show, but Adrian was loose, easy.

Packer went through the steps in his mind as Adrian did them physically. *On the rails, rope up. Knees down to let him know you're coming. Slide down, nice and easy, not too much pressure, don't want him to crouch. Rope up, pass around the hand, tighten 'er up.*

He heard Adrian's knuckles creak, the rosin groaning as he humped up off his pockets. Packer counted in his head. Adrian had an internal timer of sorts. Ten, nine, eight… Those eyes met the gate puller's at five, shoulders rolled at three, then that chin nodded. Bingo.

Packer stepped back to watch Adrian ride, almost holding his breath.

The bull kicked and spun, going against Adrian's hand. The man spurred like a bitch, heels going like a wild thing.

He knew Adrian counted in his head again, only needing eight seconds this time. There. That was it. Now off.

Easy as pie, Adrian's butt hit the dirt, Pharris caught the bull's attention, and Nate got Chook up and moving.

Bingo. He gave Adrian a double high-five when he climbed the chute, grinning like an idiot.

"We're getting that dress on her. Swear to God," Packer said.

"You know it, Pack." Adrian whacked his shoulder before going down to salute the crowd and get his rope.

The man had his hand on his phone before he was all the way through the gate, that text from Calleigh coming in. His phone buzzed about a second later and he grabbed it.

Looking hot, P.

He grinned. Maybe preened a little. It was good to hear.

Adrian was all grins as he headed over. "Not bad, eh?"

"Not bad at all, Chook. Eighty-nine points." Hot damn.

"You know it. I got motivation." Little shit.

"That is some serious motivation."

"You know it." Adrian's grin was pure horny devil.

Packer grinned and copped a feel when someone pushed past them, knocking them together.

"Oi!" Adrian hooted, leaned against the fence, eyes on the arena. "Gonna make the short go this time."

"Mind in the middle, Chook." That was all Adrian had to do.

"I got it. I want that girl in that dress for us."

Privately, Packer thought she'd wear it even if Adrian didn't win, but who was he to harsh the lad out?

Kynan walked by, gave him a grin. "You did survive! I owe CB a beer."

"Well, make sure he buys the good stuff."

"How long you out, man?"

"'Nother few weeks, maybe three." Doc had said four, but he was doing therapy.

"Bummer. Hate waiting. Adrian, you want to ride with me to Phoenix? Cotton's always with his girl now."

"Let me see, huh?" Adrian nodded, bouncing a little.

Pack hid his grin. Right. There was going to be him and Calleigh in Adrian's big black truck, teasing the little fuck until he begged. Adrian was being polite, though. Go him.

His phone beeped again. Calleigh teasing him about being horny. Playful sheila.

He had an evil idea taking a picture of Adrian's ass framed by the chaps and sending it on. The return text came back almost immediately.

Uhn.

Then, about a minute later, there was a picture of her boobs, a hickey from this afternoon on one. He popped Adrian on the butt and showed him the phone.

Adrian's lips parted, eyes meeting his. "What did you do with my innocent girl?"

"Huh?" Packer spread his hands. "Don't know what you mean."

"Uh-huh." He got this grin, wicked and happy.

"You ready for that next ride, Chook?" Packer was ready to ride something. Just not a bull.

"You know it. Gonna cover that bull." Adrian nodded to him. "Then we'll have our night, eh?"

"We will. We're going to tear you up, Chook. Just give us a reason."

"I will."

God help him, look at that grin.

All he had to do was wait for Adrian to make that ride, because Chook would do it, for them. Their Adrian was good that way.

Packer let himself have a handful of ass for a moment. "Can't wait to set Calleigh loose on this, Chook."

Adrian's eyes flashed up at him. "Don't you go there, now."

"No? When should I?" He thought about whispering some very naughty things, but Houston Rogers came up, and everyone held their breath, wanting the man to do well his first event back.

The kid went round and round, spinning, spurring, holding on. They all cheered when he went the eight, bounced up off his ass and dodged a mad as hell Meatlocker. Coke Pharris simply brushed the big monster off, and Nate hauled Houston up on the fence.

They slapped him on the shoulder, nodding at his huge grin. "You'll have to outride him, huh?"

"No worries." Adrian winked at him. "I got incentive."

"You have no idea, Chook. None at all."

* * * *

The music blared and Calleigh danced with a couple of the new Aussie riders, waiting for her men to clean up, come down to the party. One of the boys was blond and pretty and knew it, flirting hard, shaking his ass. Fun.

Aussies took good care of her. She grinned. She couldn't wait to see her boys. Blond and Beautiful wrapped one hand around her hip, moved her into a close hold, thigh pressing between her legs.

"Oi, mate. I don't think so." Packer came from behind her, pulling her back against his chest. "Dancing is all well and good. That crosses the line."

Oh, God. That was something else. "Pack." She couldn't stop her wiggle, her smile.

"Hello, luv. You ready to really get your dance on?" Adrian had always loved to dance with her, but Packer's ease with it surprised her every time.

"You know it." She turned, hands sliding around Packer's shoulders. "You smell so good."

"So do you." He sniffed her neck. "Though I need to rub on you a bit, get rid of the Old Spice."

"I like it." She lifted her chin, her breasts sliding on his chest.

"Mmmhmm. I don't wear it, though. Chook does, and you weren't dancing with him." Packer bent and nibbled on her neck.

"Oh... Naughty, naughty." She wanted and they'd promised her that she'd have tonight.

"Can't help it, love. You bring it out in me."

"That's not all I want to bring out in you, Pack."

"Aren't you married to another bull-rider?" The voice was snide, and she stiffened, pulled away from Pack. Damn it.

Pack frowned at the little girl, what was her name? The one who was always so awful about Adrian. Brandy. "He's about. What do you want, girlie?"

"Just wondering why you're wasting your time on someone taken when there's younger, more available girls around."

Christ, buckle bunnies could be bitches.

"Well, you put your noggin on that one, sheila." Packer put an arm around her waist, pulling her away.

She giggled softly. "That was nicely put, honey."

"Thanks, luv. Look who missed the whole show."

Adrian came up, a drink in each hand, one in the crook of his elbow. "What?"

"Pack was defending my honor." She took her margarita. "Thank you."

Adrian frowned. "From who?" He seemed ready to throw down. So cute.

"Some asshole girl. You'll get her telling you I'm cheating. Watch out." She rolled her eyes.

"Ah." His expression cleared. "Good thing we have this whole Packer thing."

"Absolutely." She leaned over and gave Adrian a long, lazy hello kiss.

Adrian moaned for her, his hands sliding down to touch her ass. He squeezed, making her gasp.

"Gonna make me spill my drink, Ades."

"Oh, now, Chook. Don't get her all wet," Packer drawled.

Adrian laughed, the sound pure wickedness. "But that's a good thing, mate."

"You smell good, Ades. Are you going to let me get back on the dance floor?" She couldn't help but tease.

"Only if you go with me." Adrian put his drink down, one hand on her hip.

Oh. Oh, yes. "I'd love that."

"Then let's go." Ades tugged her out on the floor, and to

her everlasting surprise, Packer came with them.

She grinned over. "You gonna grind it, Pack?"

"I am if you are." His hand slid down, his fingers pinching her ass.

"I am. God, I love to dance." And she was aching for it, bone deep. She needed them to take her upstairs later, love her. First they would all dance, though, which was a fantasy of hers anyway.

Adrian shook it for her, swaying in front of her, his body glancing off hers. Pack stayed behind her, pushing against her ass. Calleigh closed her eyes, arms up as she let the music take her, let it move her body. She felt sexy, slinky, but caught between them she'd never felt safer.

"Damn, sheila." Packer's voice was a growl beside her ear. "You won't be dancing like this with any other cowboys."

The words gave her a thrill, right down her spine, even her toes tingling. He was possessive, both of her and Ades. It was smokin' hot.

"You sure? Ades might like to watch." She winked at Adrian, including him in the tease.

"Then he can watch. You and me. I think he'd rather participate, though."

"I think I'd rather dance with the two of you than almost anything." Almost. Fucking won. By a landslide. Especially when she and Pack ganged up on Adrian and made him do indescribably hot things...

Adrian's eyes went heavy-lidded. "You got naughtiness in your eyes, baby girl."

She leaned in. "I want to watch Pack fuck your red ass. I want to fuck you while you suck his cock. I want you both inside me, making me scream."

Ades swallowed, his face going red even as his blue eyes went supernova hot, staring into her. "God, baby girl."

Pack's cock nudged her ass. "Wicked woman."

She turned, leaned against Adrian. "Should I tell you what I want from you?"

Packer's deep smile lines all crinkled up, and he nodded,

moving close enough that they all rubbed together. "Lay it on me."

"I want you to give it to me, take me hard." God, this was sexy, a bit embarrassing, but blisteringly wonderful. "I want to ride your mouth while Ades rides your dick. I want…" *You to love me, too.* "…everything."

Packer nibbled on her ear, his breath giving her shivers. "I want you both, too, luv. Now. We should go before I embarrass myself."

"Yeah." Adrian tucked her under one arm. "We're starting to get a little attention."

She glanced around, noting some stares. A few jealous, a few open-mouthed. Oops.

"Upstairs, hmm? We'll play." Oh, man. Nosy bitches at eleven, closing in. Fast.

"Yeah." Adrian steered her away from the encroaching crowd of females, Packer guarding the rear.

They made it to the elevator, Dillon Walsh sliding in with them, two coffees in hand. "Six please."

She pushed six and fourteen, her heart beating hard, like they'd been caught doing something wrong. Ades and Pack, though? They brazened it out.

"Oi, Dill. Nice show last night," Packer said, nodding at the clown, who looked totally different sans makeup. More like a regular guy.

Dillon grinned. "Thanks, man. Tough crowd. Had to be on my game."

"You had 'em going."

"Yeah, so did you guys."

What did that mean? She blinked from Adrian to Packer, biting her lip. Ades just chuckled. "Got no idea what you mean, Dillon."

"You both…rode." Those eyes were dancing, laughing at them as the elevator doors opened. "Have a good one."

The doors shut, and Pack and Ades both cracked up. She wanted to hit them. Hard.

"You're both shits!" People were going to explode. Two

cowboys. Two hot Aussies.

God, they were amazing. It was so hard to stay mad at them, especially when Ades bent to kiss her, his mouth hot and hungry. His tongue pushed into her lips, fucking her, hand wrapped around one of her breasts, thumb working her nipple.

Packer moaned, the sound echoing a little, but she had no idea what he'd been about to do. The doors opened and Adrian yanked her toward their room.

She stumbled along behind him, Packer's hands on her ass now, hurrying her. She thought she might break a leg on her heels, but Pack caught her when she stumbled.

"I got you." Packer was hard as stone, cock rubbing against her ass as Adrian worked the key card.

Her heart raced, her pussy so wet she was afraid she'd embarrass herself with the evidence on her thighs. Ades' hands shook, too, so she wasn't the only one.

"Now, Chook." Packer's growl brushed her jaw, tickled her as soon as they were in.

"Yeah, mate. Yeah." Adrian tore at her clothes, the cloth straining at the seams.

Their hands were everywhere, so big, so rough, so hard, and she pushed into the touches, her nipples aching, clit throbbing as someone yanked her panties off. Oh, God. That had to be Packer, bold as brass as he unzipped his jeans and pressed his cock to her ass. His hands lifted her breasts, offering her nipples to Adrian, who swooped down, sucking one in hard.

"Oh." She moaned it out, her body starting to sway, just like they were dancing again.

"Bed. Bed, Chook." Packer's fingers worked her other nipple, the pressure making her mouth dry.

"Gonna fall down if we don't," Adrian agreed.

"Can't fuck her like she needs if we don't."

Calleigh's knees went weak. The things they said made her pussy clench, her legs rubbing together to give some friction. They lifted her, both of them taking part of her weight.

She leaned her head back, Pack's lips crashing down on hers, taking her mouth. He was all spice, all hard male angles to her soft curves. Adrian pressed in from the side, joining the kiss. He was more like molasses, slow and deliberate, sweet tempered by a rough edge.

They moved to the bed, Adrian easing her down to the mattress even as she worked his shirt open. Packer slipped her heels off, then came after everything. Suddenly clothes were flying—jeans and buckles, underwear and shirts. Someone lost a button. Calleigh's nails accidently scored Adrian's belly.

"Christ," Adrian moaned, his muscles pulling up.

"Sorry." She twisted on the bed, lips on Ades' belly, tongue sliding on the little scratch.

"Don't be, luv. He liked it. Little pain slut." Packer laughed, but it was a sexual, dark, happy sound, not mocking.

"Hey!" Ades tried to protest, but it didn't sound real.

Calleigh bit, tugging the tiny hairs on Adrian's trail to glory. "Our slut."

"Yeah, love. Ours." Packer touched her, his fingers pressing between her legs from behind, dipping into her pussy. She spread, aching for it, for both of them, and she rocked back, taking those hard fingers deep, moaning in complaint as they disappeared.

"Hush, baby girl. Pack's got you."

Sure enough, Packer moved in close again, cock prodding at her folds. His hands were at her ass, spreading her, thumbs sliding against her hole even as his cock pushed inside her. She bent her head, mouth taking Adrian in deep.

He cried out, hands on her shoulders. "Fuck. Fuck, mate. Look at you two."

"She's hot, Chook. Hot and wet and so good." Packer moved, pushing forward.

Adrian's dick spread her lips, Pack's pushed into her cunt, and she shook, feeling like she was burning alive. She sucked, her breasts heavy and bouncing.

151

"Is she tight around you, mate?"

His thumbs pushed in deeper and she groaned, gaze flashing up to meet Adrian's. He smiled for her, his beautiful eyes on her, watching her every move.

"Fuck, baby girl. I want you. So fucking bad." Ades blinked at her, stared with needy eyes.

"Anything," she murmured against the head of his cock. They could have her any way they wanted.

Adrian tugged her up, pulling her right off Packer's dick so she was straddling his cock. "I'm going to take you and so is Packer."

Pack's moan sounded like the man was in pain. She understood perfectly. That had to be the dirtiest thing anyone had ever said to her. Adrian didn't give either of them the chance to argue—he grabbed Calleigh's hips and pushed inside her, thumbs working her clit.

She gasped, her hips tilting the way Adrian obviously meant them to, opening her up for Packer. Packer's fingers—somehow slick—circled her, teasing her, making her gasp. Calleigh had never thought of her ass as all that sexy until Adrian and Packer had brought up the idea. Now they seemed intent on making her notice, making her understand how they needed her.

Adrian murmured, thumbs working together against her clit, the pleasure almost pain. Packer's finger slid inside her ass, stretching her there, and she cried out, shaking in every muscle.

"Breathe, baby girl. He knows how to make it good."

She nodded, sucking in a shaky breath. 'You—you would know, right?"

Packer chuckled, moving his finger gently inside her. "All you have to do is relax, luv. Let us in."

Soft kisses brushed across her shoulders and one finger became two, the added stretch seeming so big. "Oh, God. Adrian, he's…

"I know." Adrian rocked into her, somehow managing to match the rhythm of Packer's fingers, of her need. "The first time he touched me like that, I thought I'd die. He's good, baby girl, and he'll make it right."

There was a confidence in Adrian's voice that made her heart beat faster, made her hamstrings tight. Packer groaned, free hand landing on the small of her back, fingers rubbing hard, digging in enough that she shook.

"One more finger, luv. You should see her, Chook, she's wet and pink, stretching for me. Hungry for it, our woman." Packer's voice scraped across her nerves, as much as the touch inside her, widening her hole, making her cry out. This cry wasn't pain, though, or fear. No, it was need. She was relaxing into it, letting them pass her back and forth. Pack's lips were on her neck, her shoulder, her back, moving, whispering.

"Gonna make you feel so good, luv," Packer murmured, mouth moving on her skin. "Gonna be in there, be able to feel Ades inside you."

"Oh, God. Y'all. Y'all, I'm burning up inside." She'd never needed so much. Crazy, but true.

"We'll help, baby." Adrian kissed her and Packer's fingers slid free. She knew what came next and she tried not to tense.

"Breathe, luv. I won't hurt you." That voice was right by her ear, hands warm and soft on her sides.

"I trust y'all."

"Our girl." Packer moved away for a moment, then came back, his heat tempered by a slick condom.

Adrian nodded, but he wasn't watching her. "Ours. Our lady."

That whole thing between Packer and Adrian should have made her jealous. It had, once upon a time. Now it made her pant, made her push back, begging Packer to get on with it.

"Fuck, yes. Deep breath in, now, Calleigh girl." She sucked in a breath and a pinch to her butt made it deeper than she'd intended. Adrian nodded, rolled her clit, tugging harder than normal, and she let the breath out on a sigh. As she relaxed, Packer pushed in, spreading her nice and slow.

The sensation was huge, making her feel split in two for a moment. She held her breath until Packer nipped at her neck. "I told you to breathe, luv."

"Trying. Trying."

Adrian laughed, leaned up and caught one of her nipples between his lips.

"Ades!"

"Now, I know you're not scolding him." Pack shifted, one hand coming up under her breast to help Adrian out.

The suction was strong and the way they filled her made her shake. "Oh, y'all. Boys. I need."

"We do, too. I can feel him, luv. I can feel Adrian inside you. Can you? Like we're rubbing together."

Adrian moaned around her nipple, his tongue flicking it back and forth, back and forth.

Calleigh nodded, fighting for air, their hands driving her crazy and keeping her from moving, all at once. They rocked with her, Adrian driving into her cunt, which seemed to push Packer back, then Pack would push in, moving Ades back. She could feel them, their cocks sliding together, inside her, pressing against her.

It made her eyes roll, made her so wet that even Packer was slipping and sliding easily. "Jesus, luv. I..." Packer's mouth fastened on her shoulder even as Adrian cried out, his head falling back.

She was going to explode. Dissolve into tiny bits of pleasure. Calleigh sobbed out a breath, needing so badly that she couldn't come, couldn't let go.

"Come on, baby girl." Adrian's face was all hard angles, set deep in pleasure. He touched her, pushing down where they joined to circle her clit, as Packer pinched one nipple, tugging hard. That was all she needed. She rolled, biting out a string of curse words as pleasure flooded her.

"Listen to that dirty mouth." Packer licked at the bite mark he'd left on her shoulder, moving faster, his breath coming in great gasps.

"She's a stud. Ours. Pack, I feel you." Adrian moaned, eyes closed, hips driving up.

"Yeah, Chook. Yeah. Love that." Their thrusts rocked her body, and it was Pack with the dirty mouth, now. Filthy, in fact.

Her head fell forward, landing on Adrian's shoulder. "Love y'all."

"Love you so much, baby." Adrian kissed the top of her head, but she could feel him shake, feel how close he was to the edge.

Her clit slid over his body, the sensation enough to set her off again, a little rush that left her body tight.

Packer hollered behind her, going stiff, his cock slamming into her one last time. He went over that fast, his heart thundering against her back. Adrian moaned his own orgasm out against her skin and she nodded, damn near overwhelmed.

They all rested together and she felt completely loved, protected rather than smothered.

Packer stroked her side, fingers trailing over her skin, leaving tingles behind. Adrian kissed her chin then her cheek, light, random touches of his lips.

"Pretty lady." Pack's soft words made her blush, made her smile.

"That was something else, baby. Thank you." Ades was the more direct one this time.

"Melted me. May never walk again."

"Walking's overrated, luv." Packer laughed, easing away from her, leaving her feeling oddly empty.

Adrian held her, and in a second Packer was back, heavy and solid against her, holding her, too. Packer kissed her neck, the move tender, somehow more intimate than if he'd taken her mouth. "Love you, lady," he whispered. "So much."

Her eyes went wide, filled with tears. "Oh, y'all. I'm so lucky."

"You are?" Adrian sounded a little awed. "I'm the luckiest

bloke ever."

Packer snorted. "No shit on that, Chook."

That got her chuckling, got Adrian laughing, too. God, it was good to be there between them. Loved by them.

"Somebody tell me there's going to be room service dessert."

"Oh, God." Ades made this insane noise. "I would kill for carrot cake."

"No homicide necessary." Packer actually reached for the phone, calling in carrot cake, death by chocolate, and strawberry ice cream. Bless him.

She leaned over, kissed Packer, pouring everything she had into it. She could tell he got it, because he held her against him, his mouth taking hers, his hands shaking a little when they slid down her back. They settled together, her legs draped over Ades', cheek on Packer's chest. Perfect.

This was perfect.

Chapter Eleven

Calleigh sat on the toilet. Staring.

Well, fuck.

She opened the third box, took the stick out and read the instructions. Good thing she'd peed into a cup, because there wasn't any urine left in her. The first test had two lines. The second a plus sign. This one said pregnant. Christ.

Okay. Okay.

She...

She wasn't okay. She was pregnant. What the fuck? She wasn't fertile, right? And...

Oh, God.

Calleigh dropped her head in her hands and sobbed, her entire body shaking with it. What was she going to do?

A soft knock made her start, Ades calling to her. "Baby? We're heading down for the show. Did you want to ride with us or get a cab when it's actually time?"

"I... I think I need a shower, Ades. I haven't been feeling so great." And she needed to think, to figure out how to tell them. Separately? Together? Would they be mad? Adrian never talked about having babies after that first year when they'd tried, and Packer... Well, they'd never once discussed it. Ever.

What if Adrian said he didn't want a baby? What if it had been Adrian all this time and not her and it was Packer's kid and—Oh, God. She was going to throw up.

"Are you all right?" Ades sounded worried now.

"I'm fine. Just sweaty and gross." She stood up, wiped her eyes and went to the door, opening it a crack. "Go get ready to ride. I want you and Pack to pick up fried chicken for supper — we can eat in here, together."

That way they could talk.

"Okay, baby." He pressed his face to the crack in the door, which should have been creepy like *The Shining*, but was cute instead. "See you in a bit."

"I'll be there with bells on. I love y'all. Good ride." She kissed his nose. It would be weird, but they'd figure it out, right?

They loved each other, all of them, didn't they? And they'd absolutely, one hundred percent figure something out. She had faith in that now, what with Packer saying the words. She had a feeling he never said what he didn't mean.

Or was that the hormones talking?

What if she was going out of her mind? What if it was just sex? What if she said baby and they ran?

What if…?

She was going to puke.

"Okay, baby girl. Get you some juice, you're pale as milk."

"I will." She waited for him to go before venturing out of the bathroom. Maybe she'd have some juice and a wee nap. She found a cardigan — it was chilly in October in New England, surprisingly so, and she couldn't imagine being here in the winter — and headed downstairs to the little gift shop. She could get crackers and juice there, maybe even a Sprite.

Something bubbly wouldn't be amiss.

She slipped into the elevator, texting Brittany and Packer, saying hi to one and good luck to the other, humming softly under her breath. When the door opened, then closed, she didn't really glance up as she checked Facebook, chuckling as Cotton posted a picture of his wife's little baby bump.

That was gonna be her.

"You're Adrian's wife?"

The words surprised her and she blinked up, meeting the pale eyes of Rick Bell, the brand new CEO of the league. Hell, she hadn't even known he was actually working, much less working enough to figure out the wives. "Uh-huh."

He grunted, the sound a little...rude. "I thought so."

"Calleigh Roberts." She held out her hand, offering a smile.

He shook her hand, but there was this expression in his eyes. All business. The elevator stopped on the ground floor, but he kept hold of her hand, tugging her to one side. "Can I give you some advice?"

"I. Sure." Advice about what? Christ, was she dressed weird?

"Whatever it is you and your husband have going on with Packer Stephens is your business, but I think you ought to keep it at home. Packer needs this job to stay in the States. If he got sent down for inappropriate behavior, he'd lose his visa. This is a family show at the end of the day."

Her lips parted, and she felt like she'd been sucker-punched. "What?"

"Not only that, but Adrian relies on those sponsorship opportunities to support both of you. I've had complaints, and I've tried to ignore them, but I can't condone this nonsense where the fans can see. There's a picture of the three of you dancing together with Packer's hands altogether too familiar. It's on Facebook."

She was going to throw up.

His hawk-like face softened a little, sympathy flashing in his eyes for a moment. "I'm sorry if this comes as a surprise, okay? I found when I was working at the network I used to run that the wives are always the sensible ones. Do what you want to do at home, or even on vacation, but not on the road with the league, okay?" He patted her shoulder before heading off, pulling his phone out of his pocket.

She reached behind her, fingers slapping at the up button, praying with everything she had that one of the doors would open before anyone saw her.

God, what had she been thinking? They could make Packer leave the country and Adrian would never forgive her. Never. And this was all her fault. She was the one who had come to them, she was the one who had blackmailed them into a threesome. She was the one who was pregnant.

With Packer's baby.

The doors opened with a ding and Calleigh stumbled inside, jammed her floor button and the doors shut, letting the elevator close on the buckle bunnies trying to catch it. She wasn't sharing. Not this ride.

She managed to hold it together until she got into the hotel room, deadlocking it before she bolted to the bathroom and lost it, heaving over the toilet until she was shaking. It wasn't until she was in the shower, the icy cold water pouring over her, that she knew what to do.

She had to go.

Just walk away.

Adrian could have Packer. She'd have the baby. They could all move forward. They would be hurt, but, in the long run, it would be for the best. They'd done fine without her before.

They could do it again.

* * * *

Adrian slammed into their hotel room, Packer at his heels. Damn it all, he'd known Calleigh wasn't feeling good when they'd left, she'd never shown up at the event, and now she wouldn't answer her phone. "Calleigh? Baby girl? Where are you?"

They stared at the empty bed before Packer went to the bathroom.

"She's gone, Chook. Where the hell is she?"

"Gone." Her stuff was gone—computer, purse, suitcase, phone. Gone. He grabbed his phone again, calling her, cussing when it went straight to voicemail.

It wasn't until he slammed his fist on the table and heard the clatter of her ring on the Formica that he saw the note, the tear stains muddling the words.

Y'all. Something happened. Someone caught us, and there's

pictures and I can't get Packer thrown out of the country or Adrian's sponsors gone. I'm leaving. You two ride and know I love you. I'm not coming back. I can't. You be good together. C.

Packer crowded up close to him, staring. "What? She left? Adrian?" He didn't think he'd heard panic like that from Pack since the first time Adrian had gotten hurt after they hooked up.

Adrian read the note again. Fuck. Fuck — Ace had been at the event, so had Troy, so it was either the press or the suits that had hollered at her. He handed the note to Pack, picked her ring up. She was going to have to stop losing that.

Pack made this low, hurt noise. "She didn't talk to us at all?"

Snorting, Adrian started stripping off his belt. He hadn't changed at the event. "She's running scared. She does that."

"What did we do?" Packer stared at him, so serious, so scared. "Chook, what did we do?"

He stopped on the way to the bathroom, going back to Packer, hands on those wide shoulders. "We didn't do anything to make her leave, mate. Believe me. Someone really did say something to her, and we have been acting out."

"So, what?" Packer stared at him like he'd grown a spare head. "We just say, right-o, see ya sheila, have a good 'un?"

"No. No, we track her down. No worries, huh?" He'd call her tomorrow when she'd settled herself in at Brittany's, and it would be fine.

"No worries. Right." Packer wasn't seeming like he was on board with the plan. In fact, the man looked panicky as a fractious horse who'd seen a rattlesnake. All whites of eyes and flaring nose. It was kind of adorable. "Got to say, mate, makes me wonder if you'd be this upset if I was the one gone."

"Don't be a fucking idiot, Chook. You I would just hunt down and fuck until you came back."

"Pack." He stared at his best mate, his lover. "We'll give

it a couple days, let her cool down, let things cool down. I'll call her again tomorrow, and figure out where we'll meet up. Tell her to head to your place, wait for us there after finals."

Sighing, Packer nodded, starting to work off his clothes. "I guess, yeah."

"Don't worry about it, mate. She's a bit of a drama lover. She'll be tickled when we come for her." Calleigh loved them, loved them both, and hell, they needed to focus on the ride and not her fine body. He actually had a shot at making them some good money. That was what he did, taking care of business. The heavy-duty histrionics he'd leave to his two lovers.

Packer moved a little closer, that surprisingly big body hot and amazingly bare. Someone needed some reassurance. Good thing Adrian was good at that, too.

He reached down, rolled Pack's heavy balls in their sac. "I got you, mate."

Pack's eyes went wide, then heavy-lidded, those pretty lips pursing up. "Chook…"

"Mmmhmm. I got you. Let me have you." He leaned in, nuzzled one nipple.

"Yeah. Yeah, I need it." Pack was gearing up for a hot, hard fuck. Adrian knew that expression well. He was all over that. He hated thinking about their girl, traveling, upset. He needed to forget, too, for a little while.

Packer grabbed the back of his head, dragged him up, tongue-fucking his mouth with a wild desperation. He opened right up, letting Packer in, knowing he could take what his lover dished out. They stumbled back until Adrian slammed against a wall, Packer jerking against him.

He pulled at Packer's ass, squeezing the firm muscles. Their cocks rubbed together through his jeans, hot as fire.

"Tell me it's going to be okay, Chook."

"It's going to be okay." He pushed back, making Packer work to keep him in place.

Packer grabbed his hands, tugged them up, and he didn't

fight it too hard. That collarbone was still tender, he knew. He leaned his head back, offering his neck, his Adam's apple bobbing.

"Oh, Chook." Packer leaned in, bit at him, careful not to bruise.

"Just do it where it won't show, mate." He wanted the bright little pain Packer could give him.

Packer groaned, shoved his shirt aside and tugged the neck of his undershirt so hard the seams creaked before those lips grabbed a bit of his skin and pulled.

"Fuck, yeah, Pack." He pushed his hips forward hard, knowing the cloth covering him would frustrate Pack to death.

Pack rocked into him, rocking hard, teeth making his skin burn.

"I'm not naked, mate." He groaned the words out, his hips shaking like he was dancing as he tried to get some kind of touch.

"You noticed." Packer wasn't slowing down at all, laughing at him.

"I did. My hands, Pack, Let me have my hands." He didn't really expect Pack to let go, but Packer did like him to beg.

The only answer he got was another bite, then Packer spun him around, grinding against his ass. His hands smacked against the wall when Packer let go, and he leaned forward, resting his cheek against it so he could reach down and struggle with his jeans.

Packer did the same, and Packer's hard cock rubbed between his cheeks, sliding along the crease of his ass.

"That's it, Pack. Need that in me. Come on. Please."

Two spit-slick fingers pushed into him, drove into him, scraping like he needed. He went up on his toes, his ass pushing back, opening up for whatever Packer wanted to do with him.

"Crikey, gonna eat you up, Chook. Fine arse." Pack finger-fucked him as the other came down with a pop, warming his butt.

"God. I'm good. Fuck me, Pack. Need it." He needed everything.

The hard, rough press of Packer's cock made him hiss, push back, the raw scrape of it soothing his nerves. Crazy, how that worked. Adrian moaned again, panting, cock so hard he could have drilled a hole in the wall.

"Love." The single word hung there for a second, then Pack started humping him hard, driving into him.

Yeah. They were— This was definitely love. Packer was his and Calleigh's. Adrian pushed back, slamming back, forcing Packer deeper. The burn made him cry out, made him buck like a rank bull.

One of Pack's hands pushed between him and the wall, fingers wrapping around his cock. That calloused hand made him groan, the pleasure going through him like lightning.

"Come on. Come on, now. Give it to me." That hard dick pegged his gland, Pack's thumb pushing at his slit, and Adrian lost it, his spunk spilling out all over the damned place.

Packer bit his shoulder, hips rolling restlessly, losing the rhythm. All he had to do was clamp down with his muscles, squeezing Packer as tight as he could.

"Chook!" Heat flooded him, filled him, Packer jerking into him.

He leaned against the wall, panting, his breath shallow and fast. "I needed that."

"Uh-huh. Tell me we're going to fix this with her."

Adrian fought not to roll his eyes, then gave in to the impulse when he realized Pack couldn't see. "I promise. We'll have her back in no time."

"Okay, Chook. I believe you."

"You'd better," Adrian said. Packer slipped away from his body and Adrian turned, grabbing Pack and kissing the man hard. "I'm a man of my word and you know it."

"I do, Chook." Packer shook his head. "She's under my skin, hmm?"

"You love her like I do. I got to admit, I'm glad."

"It's hard not to." Packer grinned. "We're good, yeah? The three of us."

"We're good, mate."

He believed it with everything in him. Now all he had to do was get Calleigh back on board.

It wouldn't take much, not really. Hell, she needed everything to calm down.

* * * *

Packer stared down at Pollyanna's broad, brindle-colored back and thought about just cutting and running. The bull ate cowboys for breakfast, not tossing them to the ground, but head-butting them first. God knew he hadn't stayed on a single bull at the finals in three rounds, and now he'd pulled this monster beast.

He thought he might upchuck.

His bull rope was on there, though, and Adrian stood right there next to him, chattering at him in that half-Aussie, half-American voice. "Come on, mate. You can do this, yeah? Flat out like a lizard drinking, that's how you need to ride."

He tried hard not to glare at the man. What he needed was his life back together. Eight weeks Calleigh had been gone, and she didn't just not answer her phone. She'd changed her number.

When she' said gone, she'd meant it, and his best mate was acting like it wasn't nothing, like they'd keep on riding and traveling and drinking piss-light beer in shitty hotel bars. Packer knew better. The ache in his belly got worse every day, the whole balance thrown off. It was why he couldn't ride.

"Pay attention, Stephens!" Nate snarled at him through the fence, glaring. "I swear to God, you asshole, either ride or get out of the chute."

"Shit. Sorry. Sorry." He needed to ride. Needed to do something to make some money. He and Ades would need all their bloody resources to find Calleigh. He got settled, got his hand tight in the rope, and looked at Adrian for long moments, those blue eyes staring into his.

Then he nodded.

The bull jumped, the world spinning wildly around him for a breath before Pollyanna started bucking, throwing his big-assed head down, trying to throw Packer's arse off. Packer clung to the rope, using his legs for balance, keeping his chest up and his free arm back. *Don't get pulled down. Don't get pulled down.*

"You got it. Hold on, Packer, you Aussie bastard!" Nate was yelling, and so was Coke Pharris, encouraging him.

His hand tried to pop out of the rope he was leaning so hard, but he gritted his teeth, listening to Adrian scream the countdown. "Six! Seven! Eight, Pack! Unload!"

His hand uncurled, the whole rigging popping off as Pollyanna's front end went down, hard. He curled up and went flying, crashing into Fred's arms like a lover. That stocky fellow Aussie tossed him over one shoulder and ran for the fence, Pollyanna's breath hot on his ass as he went over to land in the chutes.

Coke Pharris streaked by like a shot, grabbing a horn and tugging hard. Nate's shoes landed in front of his face, then there were hooves. The boys on the fence finally hauled his ass up out of all that dirt and metal, and he fell behind the chutes like an overturned tortoise.

The crowd was screaming, the lights and alarms going off, and Adrian's hand was there, held down to him. "Good ride, mate."

"Good on me." It was about time he did something right. Maybe the tide was turning.

"Ninety-three point four, mate. Up. Wave."

Packer got up, searching for his hat to wave. He didn't find it, so he stuck his hand up in the air. Coke whistled, then his hat came flying up toward him and he caught it, popped it on. Better. He hated facing the crowd all naked-headed. His ears flapped in the wind.

The crowd stopped roaring for him, and he ducked back behind the chutes area, flipping out his phone, hoping against hope there would be a text from Calleigh, a 'good ride' note.

Nothing. Damn it.

Damn it.

The excitement from the ride disappeared with a pop. How could he miss her so fucking much? He'd accepted needing and loving Adrian a long time ago, and against his better judgment at that, but how had Calleigh made him care so damned much?

Fucking woman.

Fucking rules.

The cameras came at him and he shook his head, heading back to the dressing room. He didn't want to do that, damn it. Hell, right now he wasn't sure he wanted to do any damned thing.

One of them bitchy sheilas followed him all the way down the long hall, closing the dressing room doors behind her. "You look like you could use a massage, cowboy."

"Oi, you can't come back in here. Riders only."

"I'm here. Look, she's gone, you know? She's married to someone else. I'm not. I could make you feel good."

"Any idiot with a pair of hands could make me feel good. Doesn't mean I'd touch you with someone else's dick." He found his phone and dialed security.

"You asshole. You think I won't tell my daddy that you did something to me? Touched me?"

"You tell him whatever you want, you little mongrel. Daddies know when their girls are sluts."

"Coming, sir. Please stay on the line — we're recording." That was handy.

The little gal gasped, then turned a bright, deep red. "You fucker!"

"Piss off." He pushed past her, unlocking the door for Chad, who had his phone out, listening to their conversation.

He rolled his eyes and stomped back out to the chute to

find Adrian, someone. Maybe he'd punch the fucker in the nose and tell him they had to go find their woman.

"Packer! Great ride!" The bird with the camera caught him, grabbing his arm with her talons. "Talk with me a moment and tell us what you did to get that score."

He ground his teeth. "I held on."

She laughed with her mouth, but her eyes were flashing furious. "Ha ha. Cowboys. You've been in a slump — is it too late in the season to recover?"

"Well, it's the finals, yeah? Unless I can win the event title I'm pretty screwed." He wasn't in the mood to play.

"Oi, Packer! Mate! Need you to pull rope!" Adrian's voice cut through the noise.

He summoned up a creaky smile. "That's my cue. G'night."

He swung up, arching an eyebrow at his Chook's grin. "Seemed like you were fixin' to blow."

"I was. All over her. That little, two-toned buckle bunny tried to molest me in the locker room." He ran a hand over Ades' butt, but no one could tell in the press of bodies and cables and fence.

"Fuck, she's a stone cold bitch. I bet she got to Calleigh."

"You think so?" Pack honestly thought Calleigh could hold her own with the chickies. It was the suits who intimidated their girl.

"Maybe. I don't know." That was the first crack he'd seen in Adrian about this, but then Chook shook it off. "I got to ride, mate."

"I know. Keep your chin down, chest up. Turbo is an honest bull, Chook. You can spur him to a ninety at least."

"I'm gonna be in the money." Focused little fuck. Had he been like that? Really? Adrian was all about the next bull.

Packer was starting to think he was all about settling down. Weird, huh? He nodded for his Chook, though. "Of course you are. Just don't let him get you back on your arm."

Adrian grunted, bouncing from side to side, light on his

boot heels. Ah, cowboy calisthenics. They'd always been one of Pack's favorite things to watch, and Adrian's ass was legendary.

He got a grin — warm and wild, ready. "Let's do this go-round, mate. Aussie Aussie Aussie!"

Packer hooted. "Oi, oi, oi."

Sliding over the rail, Adrian pushed gently down on Turbo's back, digging his hand into the rigging. Boom. Packer hopped up and crossed the rail, going to pull the tail of that rope as tight as he could.

He could hear Fred, yammering at Adrian through the gate, talking hard and fast, saying the things he'd say if he wasn't tugging so hard he couldn't breathe. Fred was a good 'un, though, and always watched out for his brothers from Oz.

Adrian's rope got set and he climbed over, nodding at Cotton, who had one hand in Adrian's vest. Cotton's freckled hand always seemed so weird among all the dark tans, and it made him smile for the first time in days. Really smile.

Adrian saw him and grinned, looking for all the world like a goofy, hat-wearing monkey.

He laughed, winking, and that was when Adrian nodded, the gate swinging open.

Turbo did his job, so did Chook, and so did the bullfighters. It wasn't a stellar ride — Turbo was only a couple of years from retirement, but Troy loved the big old beast — but it was a ride, and eighty-six point six wouldn't hurt. Not the way Adrian was riding this damned finals.

Packer high-fived the man when he climbed over the fence instead of going around through the gate. "Good deal, Chook."

"You know it." Adrian was all grins. "You staying for the signatures?"

He shook his head. "I did the meet and greet before. Don't have to."

"Then let's go!" Adrian tugged his arm, heading off to the

lockers.

Pack kept a sharp eye out for little birds who didn't belong back there on the way. Security was standing back there, solid and glaring, and he nodded. Fucking A. AJ was there, now, too, and Biscuit.

"We're fixin' to head to the steakhouse. Y'all wanna? It's off the main route, so the crowds shouldn't be there." AJ did his damnedest to avoid the fans when he wasn't working.

He glanced at Adrian. There was still nothing from Calleigh on his phone. No sense worrying when they couldn't find her until after. "Sure. I could murder a steak."

"Let us change and we'll be there."

They headed in, stomping off their riding boots, their sponsor's shirts. Adrian glanced at him sideways. "You better now, mate?"

"Trying to." He met Adrian's eyes. "I'm going to announce, Chook." It came out, just like that. Huh. He'd thought it would be harder.

Adrian put a hand on his shoulder. "Makes a difference, when you've set your mind. I could see you were calm."

"I am. I just. You know." He was older now and he was sore. Then there was their girl. His ranch. Sleeping in a bed that was his and big enough for three.

"What about your visa?" Worry shadowed those pretty eyes for a moment. Then Adrian shrugged. "We'll figure on it, yeah? We can do anything."

"We're smart dogs, and I'll talk to Ace. He'll help me make sense of it." Ace Porter had a way of making shit work.

Adrian brightened, pulling on his show boots, the work boots in a bag. "That's the ticket. It'll be right odd."

"A-yup." He got dressed. Two more nights. Two more, then he was going to make Adrian find their sheila. Then he was going to take her to his ranch and fuck her until she couldn't walk away from them ever again.

First, though, steak. Steak and beer.

He had a ride to celebrate.

* * * *

"Hey, Calleigh. How you doing, honey?" The floor nurse came over, patted her shoulder, and it was all Calleigh could do not to cry. Adrian had won the event, the whole final event, and Packer had taken round four. That meant celebrating and laughing, playing and dancing, and she hadn't even gotten to text them.

Say congratulations.

"I'm good. Hormonal."

And fat. Five months along and she looked like she was having twins, which was still up in the air. One appointment there was one heartbeat, the next two, maybe. As soon as she could afford the ultrasound, she was finding out for sure.

Twins.

Her and her tiny apartment in the middle of Arlington, looking out over Six Flags. Goodie.

"I read that your husband did well at his event."

She nodded. She hadn't been able to lie. Three of the girls in the unit were fans and keeping lies just... Well, shit, she knew it complicated things. She'd told them the barest bones. Ades traveled, she was pregnant, he needed to ride. From there, everyone made their own assumptions.

"Well" —Sandra leaned in, whispering— "wanna go get a Sprite down at the break room?"

"Yes. God, yes." She blinked at her boss. "The ultrasound is next week."

"It'll be fine, honey. It will." Tugging her arm, Sandra pulled her away from the blinking cursor she'd been staring at.

They'd been incredibly decent to her, letting her work four tens, letting her have the patients closest to the nurses' station so she had a place if she got sick. It was a good job, a good place, and she knew she should be grateful. Not that it stopped her from bawling and wishing. She missed Adrian and Packer so bad.

She put a five in the Coke machine, got her Sprite, and stood, breathing in through her nose, out through her mouth.

"Oh, honey. Come on and sit down." Henrietta from Cardiac came over, leading her toward the break room. "It's quiet tonight."

"It is. Thank goodness. How are your kids, honey? They feeling better?"

"Mmm. They're eating chicken soup by the gallon, but I think it's that they like those noodles you gave me."

"Oh, good. I'm glad they worked." The baby — or babies — rolled and shifted inside her.

"They loves the stars." Henrietta opened the door to the break room, holding her elbow while turning on the lights with the other hand.

"Surprise!" The whole crew was there — balloons, cake, presents, a banner that said *Baby(ies) Shower.*

"Oh, y'all. Y'all." She burst into tears, so pleased. These women were so down to earth, so kind, and she had no idea what she would do without them.

"Happy shower!" Kayla, the unit secretary, came over to kiss her cheek.

"Thank you. Oh, God. Look at this!" They led her to the place of honor, handed her a corsage.

"Hey, you're going to be going on leave soon. We had to."

She nodded, giving hugs, squashing the little voice in her head that said that it was going to be impossible, paying for daycare for two, even in that tiny apartment. She'd chosen this path to give Adrian and Packer a safe road. Now she had to put on her big girl panties.

She had friends, a job, a best friend, and at least one healthy baby — she had more than a lot of people.

She just... She sure wished that she had her boys, too.

Chapter Twelve

"No? Thank you. Yes. Thank you." Adrian hung up and stared at the phone. They'd been at Pack's place for a week, there was no bull-riding for two months, and Adrian was starting to despair.

Calleigh's best friend had been cryptic at best. "If you can find her, she's not mad at you. I would be," was all she'd said before she hung up.

So, he'd started calling hospitals. His baby girl was still a nurse. Amarillo. Austin. Corpus. Now Dallas Metro. Jesus.

Irving. Grapevine. Rowlett. Allen. McKinney.

Arlington Heart Center was where he got lucky. "Oh, honey. She's on her rounds. Can I give her a message?"

"Uh." He was shocked into stupidity for a moment. "No, ma'am. I'll come on by if she's on shift for a bit."

"Is this her husband? I know she's been missing you, worrying. Poor thing, at the shower the other day she cried and cried. So hard, having your spouse on the road all the time."

"Shower? You—you had one?" He knew he sounded like an idiot, but what would Calleigh be having a shower for? She was married already.

"We did. We know that there's a good chance she won't be able to work too much longer, so we wanted to celebrate, eat cake. She loved the diaper cake we did."

Diaper. Nappies? What the hell? "I'm sure she was tickled. I've been so far out of cell range…"

"Well, I can tell her you're on the way, unless you want to surprise her? Her shift's over at three."

"Oh, I'd like to surprise her." Spank her. Lock her in

the bedroom for the rest of her life. "I'd hate to get her all excited, too, in case something happens. I'm a few hours out on the road."

"Right. Right. I'll make one hundred percent sure she's out on time."

"Thanks. I really appreciate you ladies taking such good care of her." Adrian poured on the Aussie for a moment, hoping it would be enough to make the lady on the other end of the line flutter a little. That always worked in his favor.

"You're more than welcome. Safe driving." He got a giggle and a chuckle. Bingo. That worked like a charm.

Adrian hung up, and stared at the phone again for a while. For a completely different reason.

Then he went to find Packer, who was out in the corral working a colt he'd bought a few days ago.

Okay, this was going to be interesting.

Or disastrous.

He took a deep breath, filling his nose with the scents of horse and hay. Pack looked good, old jeans and boots covered in dust, a smile on his face. Adrian hooked a foot on the bottom rail of the fence.

"We need to talk, mate."

Packer blinked over at him, frowned. "What's wrong? Did you find her? Is she okay?"

"She's in Arlington." He held up a hand when Pack dropped the lead and started toward him. "You need to cool him down and put him away, yeah? I'll see you up at the house."

"When are we leaving? What's in Arlington? Where the fuck are you going, Chook?"

"Put the colt up, Pack. We need to *sit* and talk."

"Tell me she's okay, first, God damn it."

"She's fine, mate." Adrian waited until he knew Pack could barely hear him before adding, "She's pregnant." Then he went back into the house, waiting for Packer to take care of the horse and join him.

Packer stood there like he was rooted into the ground until Froggie nibbled on his shoulder, soft lips plucking at the cloth of his shirt. He jumped, swearing when the colt skittered back.

"Sorry. Sorry, darl'. I know, huh? You've worked hard today," he murmured to the colt, his voice low, steady as he walked the silly beast in slow circles to cool him down.

Pregnant. Christ. What was—? Did that mean he was out on his arse? It was one thing for Chook to share his wife when they were all free to play, but with a baby on the way...

His mind raced. He rubbed the colt down, got Froggie a tiny bit of feed and water, and got him secure in his stall. Then he pelted up to the house, bursting in on Adrian in the kitchen, making bloody coffee.

"What the fuck?"

"She's having your baby." Adrian met his eyes, clear and direct. He couldn't read anything there, good or bad. "They've already given her the baby shower."

"My baby? Chook, I don't understand." His heart started to kick against his ribs even harder, more mule than pony now.

"I'm shooting blanks, mate. You know that. You... Well, looks like you're not."

He sat at the kitchen table. "Can you make tea, too?" He could use a cuppa.

"I can. Damned Aussie." Adrian winked at him, but the man seemed worried. "So, you want to come with me to get her? If you don't, I... Well, I don't fucking know what I'll do. Probably beat you into the dirt."

"Not come?" He was gobsmacked anyway, but for Ades to think that? "Am I such a dick, Chook?"

"You seem so...bloody ropeable."

Nah, he wasn't angry, just...stunned. A baby. *His* baby. Oh, Lord. He started laughing, then he was whooping, slapping the table. "What—what if it has my jug ears?"

"Then we call it Dumbo and, if it's a girl, we don't cut her hair." Adrian was grinning like a monkey. "A baby, mate. We're gonna be dads, eh?"

Dads. Him and Adrian. Hell, yeah. His Chook and him were gonna be dads. Packer thought he might explode. He hopped up and went to Adrian, hugging the man hard. "We are. Christ. We need to go get her."

"She gets off work in four hours. It'll take us three to get there."

"Then what are we waiting for?"

Adrian chuckled. "Tea. Coffee. A little food."

"Our sheila is in Arlington, alone." There could be...drug dealers. Drug dealers. Gang members. Germs. She was at a hospital. MRSA.

"She's safe, okay? She works at a heart center. Those places are wicked clean." Adrian kissed him, hard enough to stun him. The man did turn off the kettle and the coffeepot, though.

"Clean enough that you want our baby there?"

"Well, no, but I'm trying to be reassuring. She's always been a nurse." Adrian flapped a hand next to his face, making 'you're crazy' motions.

"Good, she'll know what to do to take care of you when you come home hurt."

"Does that mean you're going to hurt me now or that I'll get hurt on the road without you?"

Either way, it was gonna happen, especially if they stood there yammering. "If you don't get your ass in the truck so we can pick her and her shit up, I'm going to beat you down, Chook."

"Promises, promises." Adrian kissed him again before going to grab their go-bags. Christ. He'd have to call Rob Cartino to come take care of the animals again. Just for another night or two. Then their girl, and their baby, would finally be home.

Home.

Packer grabbed his phone. God damn, they'd get that girl home and he wasn't ever letting her run again.

* * * *

"You fixin' to go home, sugar?" Nanette gave Calleigh a smile, a nod.

"You know it. I'm wore out." Everything hurt, everything was tired, and she needed a long, hot bath, a chocolate bar, and to catch up on *Bones*.

"Well, get on home, you. You look peaked. You eatin'?"

"I am. It's been a long couple of days."

"Well, you have some good time off. You got some comin', huh?"

"Yeah. More than I can afford, soon. There's a cold front coming. You stay warm." She grabbed her hoodie, wrapped it around her as best she could. She'd work Thanksgiving weekend, then the doctor said she was probably going to have to stop.

That was okay. The way her ankles were swelling, she didn't want to be on her feet any longer than she had to.

She gathered her bag, waving at Natalie on her way to the elevator. Maybe she'd stop by Popeyes and order three large orders of onion rings and a chocolate milkshake. Did they make chocolate milkshakes at Popeyes?

The parking lot was cold and windy, and she listened to her shoes on the concrete, trying not to feel weird. Like someone was watching her. She pulled her jacket tighter around her, speeding up, bee-lining for her baby truck. Calleigh got there, fumbling with her keys, when two men stepped out from behind the next row.

She jerked, dropping her keys. "Damn it."

Calleigh reached down, stepped on the keys, covering them with one foot and grabbing her phone.

"Shit, baby. Are you trying to get mugged?"

Her knees bent at opposite angles, and she almost went down. Adrian.

"Oh, God. Y'all scared me." Oh, God. Oh, God. There was no hiding the baby bump, no denying what was up. She bent down, carefully, getting her keys. "What...? What are you doing here?"

Wasn't DFW big enough to hide in? How had they found her?

"What do you think we're doing here, luv?" Packer stepped up, mouth set in a hard line. "We found you, and you're coming home."

"I..." She blinked up and her boys both reached down, helping her straighten. "I can't. You two need to go to the ranch. I have my own place."

Adrian grinned, seeming way less worried than Pack. "No, baby. It's time to quit running. Packer announced his retirement at the finals and Ace is helping him work on his citizenship."

"Retirement?" The world got a little sparkly around the edges. "You both looked so good in the fourth round."

"Thanks, luv." Packer caught her when she stumbled. "You need to talk to us. Not just disappear. Scared me to death."

"I had to." God, they were both so fine. "You're going to get in trouble."

"We'll talk about who scared you off, later." Adrian reached for her, and she was sandwiched between them, warm and good.

It wasn't fair. Not at all. She couldn't break up with them, not like this. Cold rain started to fall. "I should go."

"With us. We'll come back for your truck." They turned her toward Packer's big truck.

"But..."

Packer's hand was on the small of her back, Adrian had her purse, one hand on her ass. No one had said anything about her belly. What did that mean? They helped her into the truck, Adrian sliding into the back with her. Packer drove.

"I... I need to go home." She had to pee.

"We're going to a hotel, luv. It's not far."

"A hotel." Somehow she was just...totally out of control here. "You got a hotel?"

"We called on the way," Adrian said, pulling her up against his side. "Wanted to be comfy."

"I… I was so proud, of both of you."

Packer glanced at her in the rear-view. "I missed your text."

"I have them in my phone." The tears were coming, soon and hard. "Y'all have to listen to me. I… I can't choose between you and they'll… They'll fuck things up for both of y'all if I don't stay out of the picture."

"Shh. You're gonna make yourself sick." Adrian tugged her in closer, hand coming to rest on her belly.

A storm of activity met his touch, feeling like there was a gymnastics event going on in there.

"Pack. Oh, mate. You won't believe this." He looked… awed. Not upset. Not a bit.

"What? What, Chook?" Packer's eyes met hers in the rear-view. "It moving?"

"Uh-huh. Like it's playing footie."

How was she going to tell them? Twins. And not Adrian's. Oh, God, she was going to be sick.

Just about the time she thought it was all over and she would puke right in Ades' lap, Packer pulled off the highway and made the turn into a hotel parking lot. A Hilton. Oh, man.

"I can't do this." She looked at them both. "I'm sorry. I can't do this. I…" Her hands covered her belly. "They're not yours, Ades, and I can't choose between you and I'm fucking things up and I'm so sorry."

Adrian grabbed her hands, holding them tight and staring right into her eyes. "I know it—they?" His eyes widened. "There's more than one?"

The tears did come then, harsh and wild, her entire body shaking with them.

"Adrian?" Packer parked, then came to the back seat to slide in on her other side. "What do we do?"

"Hold her and tell her we've got her back. Girls cry. Especially whoa hormonal ones."

Packer made this weird little noise, half laugh, half grunt, and pressed against her. "You don't have to choose, luv."

Those big hands wrapped around her, fingers meeting Adrian's. The babies started kicking and rolling — possibly because the guys were there, probably because she'd eaten Taco Bell for lunch and breakfast.

"Oh." Pack simply stroked her belly, Ades' fingers. "Oh, luv."

"When did you find out there were two?"

She shrugged at Ades. "Three days ago. I had to wait on the insurance to cover the ultrasound. They're due in March — they said if I can wait till January, they'll be safe."

Her baby girls.

Packer kissed her cheek. "Two. Good lord. Good thing there are two of us, Chook. We'll be running our arses off."

"You both... You don't hate me?"

"No, baby." Adrian shook his head. "We were worried about you. Aggravated when we couldn't find you right off. Pack went a little mad. But we don't hate you."

"Come on, now. The rain is getting worse and I want to get her some grub." Packer sounded determined, stubborn as all fuck.

"Get the brolly, mate."

She sniffled, but it was broken by a chuckle. Adrian sounded more Aussie after a few weeks off, spent only with Packer.

"You wait now, woman. We'll help you in."

She stared at Pack. "I just pulled a twelve-hour shift. I can walk into a hotel without help."

Packer stared back, deep brown eyes dark and serious. "You let us help, now. It makes us feel manly."

Adrian snorted. "Not only that, but I had to listen to the dangers of you working in a hospital with sick people and germs and slick floors and the fucking Ebola virus for three hours straight."

She stifled a giggle, but it slipped out anyway. "Oh. Poor baby."

"Bah." Packer got out, grumbling, digging up front for an umbrella. "It's not right."

She got out of the truck, hiding the sigh. She was in need of a shower and a snack, possibly a nap so she could figure out what she was going to do. Adrian held her arm, Pack covered them with the umbrella, and they walked her in.

They didn't stop at the desk, headed to a big bank of elevators and pushed the button.

"I thought you called it in?"

"We stopped and got the keys. Suspicious woman." Packer patted her butt. Not hard, which was good. She might pee.

"We're on the sixth floor." Adrian had her step in, hit six. "We're going to have to have a talk, baby girl."

"If you're going to break up with me, I don't want to talk."

Packer growled, the sound remarkably animal-like. "Stop it. You left, not us. We're not here to break up. We're here to bring you home!"

"I had to!" The elevator doors opened. "They were going to send you back to Australia!"

"I just wish you'd talked to us, is all." Adrian slid the key card in the door when they got to the room, five doors down the hall. "I guess I didn't give you much reason to over the years, but we'll have to make a pact or something to do it now."

"I didn't come into this to fuck it up. I just... I have to pee."

She ran for the bathroom. Oh, God. It was getting harder and harder to hold it when it was time to go. When she was done she sat there, her mind racing, until Adrian knocked.

"Baby? I have a warm robe for you."

"Thank you." She sat there, tears on her cheek, staring down at her belly, pushing against the dark blue scrubs that were dotted with raindrops and teardrops.

"Come on, baby. Pack is ordering room service and we're going to cuddle and do nothing more strenuous than watch cartoons for an hour or so. I promise."

She stood up, flushed, washed her hands, opened the door. Ades helped her take her top off and she heard them both gasp. Her hands spread over the swollen, heavy bump.

"No, luv." Packer came close, too. "No hiding. It's different, is all."

"It's amazing." Adrian took Packer's hand, brought them both to her belly, sliding over her skin.

Tears kept coming and going, like waves at the beach. She didn't know what to do. Packer scooped her up, carried her to the bed and started taking her bra off.

"Pack!" Adrian sounded shocked.

"What? She's wet, cold." Packer kept stripping until she was bare, then wrapped her in the robe. "She's preggers, not dying."

She noted that his hand was still inside her robe even after they settled, fingers stroking her belly. Someone was maybe a little obsessed. Maybe a lot.

"They're girls. Identical."

"Oh, God. They will have to have long hair, Pack."

She stared at Adrian, who was laughing like a loon.

"Oi! You don't talk about our babies that way!" Packer leaned down, mouth near her belly. "Don't you listen, eh? Your dad there, he's a bit of a chook, but a good'un. Me, now, I'm solid as stone for my girls."

Calleigh was going to fall apart. She'd fallen at work and hit her head or something. Maybe there was a hidden camera.

"Breathe, baby girl." Adrian sat down next to her. "Just lean back and let us love on you."

"I don't know if I can." She gave them a watery smile. "I'm losing it, I think."

"You can." He helped her settle, fingers brushing through her hair. Packer was kissing her jaw, her temple.

"I don't want to. Crying makes my belly hurt." She knew. She'd done it a lot.

Packer kissed her neck. "Then don't, luv. Just float a while. It can help to relax."

She managed to doze, to be safe and quiet and warm for a minute. It was the smell of steak that woke her, her stomach growling.

"Someone's hungry." Adrian got up and went to the rolling table the food sat on, uncovering plates.

"It smells good." She sat up, and she had to admit, she felt better.

"We got ice cream, too. Pack put it in the fridge."

They'd gotten a little bit of everything, from steak to salad to a big chicken sandwich.

She nibbled here and there, then she hit the mashed potatoes and moaned. Oh, God. So good. Better than Taco Bell, for sure.

"Bingo!" Packer clapped his hands, looking pleased.

She ate all of them, then stole Packer's French fries. By the time she'd eaten all of Adrian's croutons, she felt almost human. It was good, to be calm for the first time in weeks.

"So, we stop and get potatoes on the way home." Adrian grinned. "And good bread and milk?"

She nodded. "God, please."

"There you go." Pack finished off his sandwich. "Ice cream?"

She nodded. "I'm so fat." But it sounded so good.

"You're pregnant with twins!" They both said it at the same time, so offended she had to laugh.

"I am." She patted her belly. "I only have a few weeks left before the doctor says I'll have to stop working."

"Well, good thing you're coming home with us."

"Oi, does that mean no sex?" Packer asked, utterly horrified.

"Nope. I can have as much as I want. I bought a vibrator."

Now Ades was the one to look shocked. "You could have just come home!"

"I was trying to protect you two!"

"Now, kiddies." Packer sighed, putting the dishes away on the cart so they could all sit on the bed. "I'm retired, luv. It's not an issue anymore."

"How can we do this?" she whispered the words. "People are going to hate them."

"Why would they do that, baby?" Adrian petted her leg. "Why would anyone have a problem?"

"Because people suck. They don't understand that I can be in love with both of you."

Packer's eyes glittered, his lips curving in a luscious smile. "As long as we understand, it's all good. Come here and kiss me."

"What?"

"Come kiss me. I need my girl." He hauled her into his lap. "Need you, Calleigh girl. We both need you."

For a moment she felt heavy and off balance, but then his mouth closed on hers and she couldn't think of anything but Packer. Him and Adrian. The kiss started slow and soft, but it only took a few moans before he was devouring her, leaning her back into Adrian's chest.

Adrian was solid as a rock, his hands exploring her, testing all of her new curves. When his hands cupped her breasts, they all moaned. She was a little shocked at how sensitive they were, at how good it felt when he brushed the nipples. She arched, rocked between them, crying out her pleasure into Packer's lips.

"Fuck, mate. We might make her come just from this." Adrian squeezed a little, his hands pressing her breasts up.

Her pussy ached, her belly going tight, and when Adrian took her nipples between forefinger and thumb and tugged, sweet and slow, she shuddered. "Oh, please."

"Oh, we are going to have fun with this." Packer's smile had slipped back into wicked. That man couldn't stay somber to save his life. God, she loved him and that amazing grin.

"You know it, mate." Adrian's mouth was on her shoulder, teeth nibbling. "Oh, baby girl, we missed you."

"We did. Every day. All night." Packer kissed the base of her throat, working down an inch at a time.

Oh, fuck. It had been months and she'd missed them like

you'd miss a lost limb. Her breasts felt heavy, her nipples aching for more attention. She got it from both of them, Adrian lifting her breasts to Packer's mouth.

"So pretty, luv." He wrapped his lips around one nipple and started sucking, pulling hard enough that she grabbed him, pulled him closer.

"Yes."

They were making her insane and they hadn't even gotten started. She knew how good it could be now, and the anticipation made it better, hotter.

She loved how hungry Packer seemed, how those lips felt, wrapped around her flesh, the rocking pressure strong and sharp and perfect. His cheekbones stood out in hard relief and when Adrian stroked her breast and Packer's mouth, it was as erotic a sight as she'd ever seen.

Adrian's denim-clad leg pushed between her thighs, giving her something to bear down on, to move against, although she didn't need it. She needed them, their desire. Calleigh could smell them, deep and musky and male. Packer was more earthy, Adrian more spice.

"So fucking wet." Adrian started working her other nipple, finding Packer's rhythm and trying to kill her with it.

"I can't. Adrian. Packer. Please." Now she was begging for anything that would release the coil of tension inside her.

"You can. Come on, baby girl. Come for us like this."

Packer's lips left her nipple and she sobbed, head tossing. "Packer!"

"Shh. Just giving the other some love." He switched to the other side, which damned near made her scream.

"Look at him, so fucking hungry for you, girl." Adrian's voice buzzed over her ear and she stretched up, hips driving her wet cunt down on his thigh.

Packer moaned, licking at her skin, his hand sliding between her legs.

"Please. Please."

Packer flicked her clit and she started coming, bucking and rolling. He didn't stop touching, though. His fingers circled and rubbed, even as Adrian's hand pushed under her from behind — two fingers pushing into her pussy even as he slid his thumb into her ass.

"Oh." The noise that came out of her surprised her, almost animal in its need, in its demand.

One orgasm rolled into another and another, the pressure and pleasure twisted together, everything spinning faster and higher. She was going to go crazy if someone didn't fuck her, if she didn't have one of them inside her.

"Want you, luv. Right now." Packer pulled back, struggling with his clothes.

"Now. Now, hurry." She could feel Adrian behind her, stripping too. "Now, Packer."

"I am!" His hands were shaking, which was the sweetest thing ever.

She pulled his belt off, tugged at his jeans, offering Ades a grateful smile when he helped.

"Packer's never made love to his pregnant woman before, baby. He's a little shaken up, I think."

Packer gave Adrian a glance that could only mean amazing things for Ades' ass later on. "Watch it, Chook. Every smart-ass comment earns another spanking."

"If someone doesn't fuck me I'm going to scream." Focus, boys.

"Going to. Now." Packer was naked finally, Adrian holding her there, giving her support.

Packer pushed over her, covered her, cock sliding into her with a long, needy stroke, sending flashes of pleasure through her. His body burned against hers, new scars there that she would have to explore later.

"Harder. Need you like breathing."

"Oh, luv." Packer stared right into her eyes, pushing in and out, moving faster and faster.

Ades had her back, holding her. Those hands of his were everywhere, too, on her breasts, her belly, Pack's chest.

The need was so big—battering at her—that she groaned, driving her hips down, taking Packer's cock like a wild woman. He was just as wild inside her, pushing her higher and higher. Adrian touched them where they joined, fingers slipping against her wetness, Packer's hardness. When Adrian started circling her clit, rubbing it, she lost it, the orgasm bigger than she'd ever had, crashing through her.

Packer shouted, his hips rocking, his dick swelling impossibly in her. Then he was coming for her, wet and hot deep inside. She distantly heard Ades' soft, shocked cry, felt his heat on her hip, but she was busy flying, waves of pleasure coming and coming.

"Christ, woman." Packer eased out of her once it was all over, rolling to one side, panting with the aftershocks.

"Uh-huh." She nodded, all baby-headed.

Adrian made this weird rumbling noise she remembered from the very first time they'd been together, and she sniffed, the tears threatening again. Damned hormones.

"Shh, baby girl. We got this. We do." Adrian hand covered her belly again. "We won't let you down."

"I don't want to let you down." She was so scared. Worried for them.

"You can't." Packer kissed her. "You're our girl."

Like it was that easy. And maybe for a little while she should let it be. She was tired and sick of going it alone.

Adrian slipped away, cleaning her up before a blanket floated down, covered them.

"Come here, Chook," Packer demanded, pulling Adrian back down to them. "Gimme a few and I'll tear your arse up."

"Sounds perfect, mate." Adrian cuddled in.

It did. Perfect. Which meant something was going to fuck it up. Something always did.

Chapter Thirteen

"You've been living here?" Packer put his hands on his hips, facing down Calleigh's apartment like he would a charging bull. "This is terrifying."

"What?"

Like she couldn't see the water stains, the half put-together cribs, the... Was that a water bug? In the place where their woman and babies *slept*? No, this would never do. "I hope you still have the moving boxes."

"If she doesn't I'll go get some."

"This is my apartment."

"No, this is a shithole."

Adrian nodded to Pack, frowned at her. "Baby? You had money, you told me."

"I was already pregnant. No insurance coverage, I knew I'd be out of work for at least three months, now..." She shrugged, the expression defensive as all fuck. "I had to be careful."

"That's stupid. Christ, woman." Packer was going to beat her. "You have a home, you have two men to take care of things, and you just... Here? In this?"

Adrian held up a hand, keeping him from throwing anything. "This isn't helping." When he sputtered, those dark eyes bored into his. "I know. Now stop. We'll pack, baby girl. You sit."

"Call that damned PODS place and have y'all's stuff delivered, too." When she opened her mouth he snarled, "Now, God damn it! I will not... You are my girl. You deserve better!"

They both stared at him, Adrian grinning, Calleigh's

lips quivering, and Packer threw up his hands. "Am I not making sense?"

"You are. It's fucking adorable. You've gone all caveman grunting married family man. It's the cutest thing ever."

Packer's hands clenched with the need to strangle Adrian. Really. Dead. He was actually moving to do it when Calleigh stopped him.

"If you kill him, you'll have to hide the body, then you'll have to rock the babies alone."

'The babies'. God, he loved those words. His smile came from his toes, and he grabbed her, hugging her tight. "I'd have you. I want both of you helping me with those rugrats."

"Are you sure he's not hormonal, Ades?" Her belly pushed right into him.

"I think he's in love." Adrian moved in close, too, one hand on his ass, one on Calleigh's waist.

"Yep. In love and ready to get your shit into the trucks. Ades can drive yours, you can ride with one of us." They'd done enough dancing about. It was time to get moving. Time to go home.

"But."

"You're coming." Adrian chuckled, kissed Calleigh, and headed over to the boxes of baby things. "You have enough shit, baby girl?"

"I didn't know there were going to be two, then."

"Two babies need lots of crap." Packer started loading things into boxes, setting them next to the door.

"Leave the kitchen shit. I just want my clothes and stuff from the bathroom."

He was going to holler with sheer fucking joy. She was cooperating. It was as if she finally believed that they were keeping her, that she didn't need to choose.

"What do I do about my job? I didn't give notice."

"I'll talk to them if I need to. You were close to maternity leave," Adrian said, and it was all Packer could do not to growl. Adrian was Calleigh's husband. That was his right.

Adrian looked at him, eyes knowing. They had shit to figure out, decisions to make. He gave his Chook a smile, though—this had to be hard for him, too, but Adrian gave and gave. Packer knew he was the luckiest fool on earth.

Calleigh stretched, one hand on her back, one on her belly.

"Luv? Are you all right?" He dropped everything to go to her, helping her sit on a kitchen chair.

"I'm fine, just feeling Frick and Frack here do somersaults." She took his hand. "Want to feel?"

It was like a madhouse, rolling and kicking and punching. He couldn't imagine what it felt like for her. "Do they do this all day, luv?"

"They move a lot more than I thought they would." She took his other hand, brought it to the small of her back. "Rub."

He did, flattening his hand and pushing in a little, giving her warmth and pressure. She'd been so good to him when he was hurt, and it felt amazing to be able to give it back to her.

She relaxed, eyelids closing, and the babies eased up, too. So tense. He met Adrian's eyes, and his Chook nodded. Time to take her home, let her relax, let her breathe while they took care of things.

They would pack her shit, close down the apartment, and talk to her work people while she decorated the nursery and got off her feet.

He rubbed until she was sagging against him, blinking slow. "Have a nap, luv, and me and Adrian will get the trucks loaded."

"Are you sure?"

"Absolutely, baby." Adrian took her to lie down, and they started the process of loading the baby things and her really personal items.

They stopped together on the landing, just them. "You good, Chook?"

"I am. We'll have to work at it like we never have, you know?"

"I know." He wouldn't deny that, wouldn't pass it off as nonsense. They would have a lot of give and take.

"It's going to be fucking hard, but so fucking good, mate. Our family. I get you both—my lady and my best mate."

Packer put his box down, reaching out to give Adrian a hard hug. "I know what you mean, Chook. I love you. You know that, right?" The words got easier to say every time.

"I know." Adrian grinned, eyes dancing, as wicked naughty as they could be. "Did you see how wild she was for you last night? This is going to be so much fun."

His cock jumped a little at the thought. "You know it, Chook. I can't wait."

"Let's go take our girl home, then. It's time."

"You know it, Chook. Let's give the lady what she wants."

He followed Adrian's amazing ass back inside to get his girl, knowing that a whole new life was opening up for him, one he'd frankly thought he'd never have. Packer amazed himself by wanting that life more than he'd ever wanted anything in his life, including the next bull-ride.

Epilogue

"God damn it, Adrian! Did you eat all the mashed potatoes?"

He stared at Packer, and Packer stared right back. "Chook, is she in the kitchen?"

Calleigh was supposed to be in bed, resting. Quiet. The woman was the size of a rhino, the babies making her swollen and grumpy and hungry.

Really hungry.

"I think they're under the chicken, baby." He wandered to the kitchen door, leaning there to blink at his girl.

Tired and scowling and wearing a sweater that was the size of a tent—she'd never been so pretty. "Under the chicken. Right. Monday I get to go to the hospital and not be pregnant anymore, right?"

"That's what they say." He crossed the room to kiss her, then relieve her of her armful of cold snacks.

"Good. I'm tired, Ades. The girls are heavy."

"They'd be lighter in the bed, woman." Packer came to her, rumbling, hands searching out her sore spots. Pack was surprisingly good at the domestic thing, better than Adrian had ever imagined. Hell, he was the one sending Adrian off to ride bulls with a wave and a smile.

"I was hungry and bored and I don't want to watch any more movies. I want to be with you two."

"All you had to do was yell, you mad thing."

He and Pack grinned at each other over Calleigh's head when she growled. It was a great noise.

"Well, come and sit with Pack on the sofa while I put us some food together."

"Okay. I want…"

"Mashed potatoes. Calleigh, the man's not daft. He knows." Packer got her moving, arm around her expanded waist.

"I might want pickles!"

She didn't, though. She'd never had a pickle the whole time she'd been pregnant. Those weird crackers shaped like fish? Sure. French fries? God yes. Packer had even learned to make homemade onion rings, but no pickles. There was nothing more hilarious than Packer in a Kiss the Chook apron.

Adrian got the mashed potatoes out, the chicken and fixed her a plate, popped it in the nuker, grinning. Monday they'd have their girls and by the middle of the week they'd be in the newly painted nursery.

The timer was almost done when he heard Calleigh cry out, the sound sharp, almost scared. He'd made it to the kitchen door before he heard Packer holler, "*Chook!* Bring towels!"

Adrian didn't even ask. He just got towels, feet slapping on the floor as he ran from the laundry to the front room. His eyes widened. *Whoa.*

"My water broke."

Yeah, yeah, he could see that. Damn.

"Toss me the rags, Chook, and help her get cleaned up to head to town." Packer helped her up, got her moving. "Looks like we don't have to wait for Monday. Wednesday is a good day for babies."

Calleigh came to him, a panicked expression on her face. "Ades?"

"It's okay, baby girl. Pack and I have birthed hundreds of calves. This is the way it works." She knew that, but she had to be freaked out.

"I am incredibly comforted, Ades. Thank you." Calleigh arched an eyebrow, popped him. "Glad you're here."

There'd been a chance that he'd have missed this, if she'd gone early. As it was, they both got to be there. The most exciting moment of his life, and he got to share it with his girl and his very own cowboy.

Adrian had never been happier than when Calleigh had pressed her point that day in the hotel, making them include her. It had been the only way to make things work.

"Me too, baby girl. Come on. Let's get your clothes changed and I'll grab your ready bag. We got babies to meet."

They were going to be daddies, him and Pack. Crikey.

Good thing his girl'd got what she wanted.

City Country

Excerpt

Chapter One

"You've got to be fucking kidding me, Em."

Emily was going to beat her best friend to death. With a hammer. A dull, rusty hammer. "Oh, stop it, would you? My fucking feet are tired, Ricki, and I want a goddamned beer."

Ricki's kohl-rimmed eyes went wide as she stared at the neon sign above the club. "The Wagon Wheel. Yay."

Emily sighed and nodded, knowing this wasn't the best possible choice, but the bus didn't run for another hour and fifteen this late and Sixth Street was another hour's walk and… Hell, her feet were killing her in her thigh-highs. Really. Even with the platforms, the heels were deadly.

"I'll buy. One beer each, huh? I swear to you, the steel guitar won't kill us."

Ricki blinked, looking more and more like a raccoon with

each passing minute. "No, but the shit-kickers might."

"One beer. I'll protect you. I'm butch."

Country music types milled around out front, and a guy with worn-down boots and a big cowboy hat was perched on a stool by the door. "Ladies' night. No cover for y'all, ladies."

"Thanks, man." She grabbed Ricki around one rubber-and-lace-clad arm and tugged. "Come *on*."

Hell, if Ricki hadn't fought with Preach and Tin Lizzy, they wouldn't be hoofing it home from the rubber ball, would they? No. No, she'd be in the back of that weird-assed conversion van heading down toward SoCo.

Conversation just inside the door stopped dead when they walked in. The girls were all plaid shirt, Daisy Duke, straw hat types, and they obviously didn't like the Goth aesthetic.

"Just one beer, huh? Then we'll go." Em doggedly tugged Ricki toward the bar, her desperately tragic-looking, waifish best friend managing to dig those Doc Martens in good and hard.

"Screw it. I'm calling a cab. You're on your own, Auntie."

She was never going to live down The Wizard of Fucking Oz. Ever.

"Thanks, man. You're a pal." She rolled her eyes and let go, trying not to rejoice too hard at the way Ricki stumbled backward and almost fell. Knowing Ricki, she'd at least get her cab ride free. The skinny girls always did better that way. Em made her painful way to the bar, then propped herself up on a stool, and waited for the bartender to notice her.

As if anyone in this hick bar hadn't noticed her five foot nine, corsetted, stiletto-heeled, pink and green highlighted hair, tattooed self.

The bartender was more freak-friendly than expected, with a ponytail and a gold tooth. "Hey, darlin'. What'll you have?"

"A Shiner, please." She smiled back, propping her heels

on the rungs of the bar stool.

"You got it." He gave her a wee napkin and some nuts before heading off to get her beer, which was when she noticed the little pod of cowboys standing off to her right.

Did they call a group of cowboys a herd? A round-up?

A posse. That was it. A posse of cowboys.

God, they were all tiny.

Her head was as big as some of their shoulders.

There was one who kept staring at her out of the corner of his eye. He was adorable, all red hair and big green eyes — that smile enough to light up Rockefeller Center at Christmas.

Edible.

Utterly, totally edible.

She was careful not to make eye contact — guys like that didn't notice girls like her — but still...

Yum.

In a totally aesthetic way, of course.

He stood as if he owned the world, hips thrust forward and to the side a little, thumbs hooked in his front pockets. He glanced over every few minutes, each look longer than the last.

"You want a glass, honey?"

"No. No, the bottle's fine, thanks." She was a girl — she knew how to work a longneck bottle with the best of them.

"Cool. You running a tab?"

"I... Yeah. Yeah, I am." She pushed over a credit card for him to run. She wouldn't have more than two.

"There you go." He left her after that to fill a bunch of froofy beer orders for a little group of cougars dressed in really tight clothes. There was no way on earth those tits were all real. No fucking way.

She glanced down at hers, which were, if not little and perky, at least firm and very well presented. Not to mention the ink and the pretty little rings that no one could see. That made her grin, made her feel settled in her skin a little more.

She was getting good at ignoring the crowd and had just

about finished with beer one when the bartender, whose name was Jib, came to check on her. "Want another one?"

She checked her watch. "Yeah. Yeah, one more. I have half an hour before the bus comes."

"I'll get this one, Jib." The cowboy had a surprisingly light voice. Not girly or anything, but the kind of voice tiny people have.

"Oh? Thanks, man. That's sweet." It was the pretty cowboy, too, with a glint in his eyes that promised pure evil.

"Sweet." He nodded, his chin strong enough to pound nails. "That's me. Soul of kindness. What's your name?"

"Emily." She chuckled. Someone had lost a bet and had to talk to the scary girl. "What's yours?"

"Cotton." He held out a square, oddly pale but freckled hand. That single hand said a lot about him. It looked like it had been through a war.

"Cotton? Like the plant?" That was rocking cool.

That hand was strong, solid. Firm.

"Yep. When I was born, my momma thought I was an albino. I had little tufts of cotton white hair." He grinned, and the world almost caved in. He had the most amazing smile ever.

"Oh, man. That is a wicked fun story." She laughed, clapping a little bit. When his eyes dropped to her chest, she couldn't help the little sense of 'score'. "I'm just named after my grandmothers—Emily Cecilia."

"I have an aunt named Cecilia. 'Course, she's Mexican." He laughed, too, nodding at the bar. "There's your beer. Want to go sit?"

"Sure, for"—she checked her watch—"fifteen minutes. I have a bus to catch."

She stood up and shook out her little skirt.

"A bus, huh?" He put the hand not holding his beer under her elbow, steering her a little. When she glanced over, his little cadre of friends were long gone.

"Yeah. I was at a party and my ride went AWOL." Sort

of. "So I walked a bit and thought I'd catch the bus home."

He was stronger than he seemed. Really.

"I could give you a ride, Emily Cecilia. Got my truck." At her raised eyebrow, he held up his beer in a defensive gesture. "No strings attached. I been on foot when the gang disappeared."

"Yeah? It's a little aggravating, especially in the boots."

"I bet. I wouldn't want you to have to ride the bus at this time of night." They sat, him waiting until her butt hit the seat to slide into the booth.

"You're sweet. Are you from around here?" Austin was one of those places where you couldn't tell, not really. All sorts of people came from everywhere.

"I'm from up north of here some." That glinting, pure-devil smile came again. "And you keep saying I'm sweet."

"You keep not proving me wrong." She took a drink of her beer, the cold bitterness just what she needed.

"Well, I'll try not to let you down." He tapped his foot, the boot toe making this neat sound. "So what do you do?"

"I design first person shooters with Fractal Monkeys." It was a great job. She'd been the secondary designer of Betty Bosoms and of Crackhead's Gang. She wasn't going to get her own game, not any time soon, but... *Right. Focus. Small talk. Pretty cowboy.* "What about you?"

More books from
BA Tortuga

Rosie doesn't date cowboys anymore, not since her husband died.

King of the cowboys, Ace gets whatever what he wants.

Addie isn't shy about hooking up with rancher Bodie, even if he has a reputation as Mr. Unlucky.

When she returns to the Texas circuit for a few events,
Kase notices something new about his ex, and he has to
know more

About the Author

BA Tortuga

Texan to the bone and an unrepentant Daddy's Girl, BA spends her days with her basset hounds, getting tattooed, texting her sisters, and eating Mexican food. When she's not doing that, she's writing. She spends her days off watching rodeo, knitting and surfing Pinterest in the name of research. BA's personal saviors include her wife, Julia, her best friend, Sean, and coffee. Lots of good coffee.

BA Tortuga loves to hear from readers. You can find contact information, website details and an author profile page at https://www.pride-publishing.com/